A YOUNG ADULT FANTASY

SEVENTH DIMENSION
BOOK 3

THE CASTLE

LORILYN ROBERTS

To Ken Kuhlken

Who taught me most of what I know about creative writing

ACKNOWLEDGMENTS

Special thanks to the following beta readers for making *Seventh Dimension – The Castle, Book 3* better than it would have been without their insightful comments:

Gregg Edwards, Kendra Stamy, Felicia Mires, and Deborah Dunson.

"Time is an illusion until God's appointed time."
—Lorilyn Roberts

INTRODUCTION

"A spiritual kingdom lies all about us, enclosing us, embracing us, altogether within reach of our inner selves, waiting for us to recognize it. God Himself is here waiting our response to His Presence. This eternal world will come alive to us the moment we begin to reckon upon its reality."

— A. W. TOZER, THE PURSUIT OF GOD.

The Seventh Dimension Multi-Award Winning Series continues in *The Castle: A Young Adult Fantasy*.

Haunted by a recurring dream of his missing father in a mysterious castle, 17-year-old Daniel is captured by the Romans and finds asylum in the temple. There he discovers a scroll that reveals his future concerning a wager between good and evil.

But the stakes are raised when he witnesses the trial and crucifixion of Yeshua Hamashiach. The convergence of time with supernatural events creates a suspenseful ending and leads to the fourth book in the *Seventh Dimension Series, The City.*

CHAPTER 1

A ringtone caused me to stumble.

"Move," an annoyed traveler mumbled.

Anxious pilgrims traipsed past me. Did no one else hear it?

The ringing continued—musical notes that blared from a rocky outcropping near the desert road. I got out of the way of others and rushed over to inspect the overhang, but the ringtone stopped too soon. Sliding my hand along the uneven shelf, I searched for the iPhone. Nothing.

I kicked the sand. Satellites didn't exist in the first century and neither did cell phones. Perspiration beaded on my forehead. How dare nonexistent technology taunt me. When I glanced down, I saw a red cellphone protruding from the dirt. It was mine, the one some thief stole from me—two thousand years in the future.

The phone rang again. ID—unidentified.

I snatched it out of the sand. "Hello."

Silence.

"Hello," I repeated.

"Where are you going, Daniel?"

Chills tiptoed up my spine. I slouched against the rocks. "Why do you torture me?"

The ventriloquist spoke in a smooth voice. "I want to help you."

The demon who had duped me into accepting a counterfeit gift when I lost God's gift wouldn't fool me again. I shouted into the phone. "No, you don't."

A woman nearby flinched.

I needed to lower my voice.

"Why are you going to Jerusalem, Daniel?"

I rubbed my eyes and wiped the sweat from my face. Crouched on the ground with my knees knocking, I spoke softly, "Why do you keep harassing me?"

"Don't go to Jerusalem."

My voice quivered. "Leave me alone."

Annoying static blared.

"Don't go to Jerusalem, Daniel."

The raspy voice made me panic. Maybe I should listen to her.

My voice cracked. "Why?"

Another passerby gawked. Only crazy people spoke to themselves in the first century.

Click.

The phone dissolved in my hand. I splayed out my fingers and stared. How could my hand be gray? In fact, tones of gray saturated the sky and everything else. I squinted.

Had the chariot accident damaged my vision? No, this must be the ventriloquist's wicked magic. She wanted me to believe I was going crazy as my family was apt to tell me. I balled my hand in a fist. "No!"

A couple of people ogled me.

An old man approached. "Are you all right?"

I nodded, appreciating his concern. I waved at the onlookers. "I'm fine."

I turned and muttered a few choice words. How many times in the seventh dimension had things not been as they appeared?

A few minutes later, hoof beats filled the dry desert air. Roman soldiers, outfitted in heavy accoutrements, led a long procession. Chariots adorned in the best Roman decor followed the horses.

Why did I have to run into Roman soldiers so soon? I hadn't even made it to Jerusalem. I was a wanted man. Travelers cleared to the sides of the road to let the peacekeepers pass.

I rubbed my eyes. The demon's wiles—I would not listen. God must be showing me something I didn't yet understand.

Because of the traffic, the Roman caravan slowed to a crawl. Fancy chariots brought up the rear. I peered inside the first compartment. Pontius Pilate sat beside an attractive woman. I laughed. The hanky dropper at the chariot races hated the Jews. How much trouble would we cause the Roman governor this spring festival?

Pesach was the only Jewish tradition my family kept in 2015. God had delivered the Jews from Egyptian slavery over a thousand years before the first century when he drowned the cruel taskmasters in the Red Sea.

The Romans took a while to pass. Precious minutes ticked by. The Shabbat meant nothing to them, but before the first two stars appeared, I needed to be on the Mount of Olives or outside the city gates.

My stomach churned. What would I give for a few figs and berries to satisfy my hunger.

I didn't relax until the Romans disappeared. I turned towards Jerusalem. I must make it to Jerusalem in time. I must. The Romans would think I had stolen the racing horses when I ran away. I hadn't, but runaway slaves didn't live long in the first century. God was my only hope. I slung my bag over my shoulder, rubbed my eyes, and walked faster.

"Please, God, heal my vision," I prayed.

CHAPTER 2

A train whistle blew. The ground shifted underneath my sandals and I felt the familiar motion of a chugging train. I gripped an overhead bar to brace myself. Cold steel walls became visible. Crowded bodies inside the car eerily reminded me of old newsreels.

Fear in the children's faces rattled me. A distraught girl around ten or eleven was crouched in the fetal position.

The smell of urine and feces almost made me gag.

A kitten lay beside the children, although the little ones seemed unaware. Young mothers cradled their cherubs in their laps.

I tried to see through the fog-covered windows. Where were we? We couldn't be in Israel—this must be the demon's shenanigans, infiltrating my mind with fear.

No one said a word. Only sobs and stifled wails from the children pierced the gloominess.

After a while, the fog cleared. A thin, fidgety woman sitting by the window shrieked, "Fire!" Heads strained desperately to see. No one said a word—terrified eyes said it all. The train continued to an unknown destination.

A few minutes later, the woman cried again, "Fire!"

"Shut up," a man demanded.

Her rants continued.

"Can someone shut up that woman?"

My eyes drifted in the direction of the voice. A few men stood in the back. How could so many bodies be crowded into such a tight space?

I peered out the window. The fog had cleared and dark clouds loomed.

A burly man wearing a cone-shaped hat, perhaps in his late forties or early fifties, climbed over several small children. He held up a dirtied cloth he had ripped from his shirt. Another man with a stubby beard and short legs followed him.

"Watch your step, mein Herr," a woman chided.

After a few tense moments and a slight tussle, the two men gagged the woman by the window. I turned my back overwhelmed with pity. When I peered at her again, a cat lay on her lap. I hoped the animal would bring her comfort.

A teen girl a row away clutched an object in her hand. She briefly relaxed her fingers revealing the Star of David. Why did she seem familiar to me?

A man and a woman began to argue in the back. Indifference had set in. No one stopped them. Mercifully, a few had drifted off.

I heard a man's voice say, "Time is an illusion until God's appointed times."

Where did it come from? The few men on the train were too far away to have said it.

The train's airbrakes released, followed by a tinny scraping as the train slowed. The cabin jerked. Hemmed bodies pressing in on one another intensified. Through the window, I saw gray brick buildings surrounded by barbwire. In big, bold letters on a rustic sign was the word "Auschwitz."

No, I cried silently. I should be in Jerusalem, not Auschwitz. The train had become oppressively hot. The woman who had shouted "fire" was either unconscious or asleep.

The door flew open and a large man with a menacing dog stepped forward. He must have been close to seven feet tall.

I stood on a dusty road. Swarms of Jewish travelers and pilgrims briskly passed me. The chatter of children playing nearby lifted my darkened spirit. The beautiful city of Jerusalem overlooked the Kidron Valley across from the Mount of Olives. Even in shades of gray, tall, impressive walls surrounded the city.

How did I go from being on the road to Jerusalem to a train at Auschwitz to standing on the Mount of Olives—before the Shabbat started?

I closed my eyes. "Thank you, God."

Selfish thankfulness tempered by the experience filled me with guilt. Was it God who brought me to Jerusalem on the train ride to hell —an illusion of sorts?

The magnificent temple captured my attention. I needed to visit the shopkeepers in the courtyard to purchase my lamb. The place bustled with activity. Throngs of people arriving for the eight-day festival had created a temporary tent city.

I noticed something shiny on the road. I picked up the small object and gently shook off the sand. The Star of David. The young girl must have dropped it. I put the necklace in my bag.

The setting sun hinted at the start of Shabbat as two stars appeared in the sky.

Suddenly a swishing sound interrupted my musings. I turned and saw a magnificent lion in front of me. Softened by self-control and inscrutable features, his perceptive eyes latched on mine. I fell to the ground and hid my face.

Nothing happened. When I lifted my eyes, life-giving color emanated from the creature. Blues, reds, and yellows seeped into the spring wildflowers. Lush green palms dotted the Mount of Olives. The gold on the temple reflected the red hues from the setting sun as streaks of crimson covered the sky. My eyes returned to the lion. He had restored color to my eyesight.

A gentle breeze rippled the lion's golden-brown mane.

The creature slunk past me and stood on the edge of the mountain. His powerful body, silhouetted against the setting sun, filled me with awe.

The lion roared. A flock of birds in a nearby palm flew away. I cowered on the ground. A few seconds later, he leapt off the mountain and disappeared. A door shut and the vision ended. I remembered the voice on the train. "Time is an illusion until God's appointed times."

"Daniel?"

I turned and saw a young boy approaching. The boy broke into a run. "It IS you—will you eat dinner with us? Simon is expecting you for Pesach."

I recognized the teen. The last time I'd seen him was almost three years ago—Mark, the young boy who lived in the leper colony with his parents. What a surprise to see him here. I wrapped my arm around him. "Yes, I'd love to join you and Simon for dinner."

CHAPTER 3

I followed Mark through the crowds. The makeshift tent city that had sprouted up next to Jerusalem must have swelled to half a million people. With the setting sun, it was difficult to see the buildings, but the temple and the massive mount surrounding it dwarfed everything else.

How had the Jews built such an imposing structure in the first century? Rome boasted of the Pax Romana. To invoke such wrath on the Jews and destroy the temple in 70 A.D. was a tragedy. The Jews never rebuilt the temple.

Mark's voice brought me back to the present. "You must be tired after your long walk from Caesarea."

I sighed. How could I explain I hadn't walked part of the way? I clutched his shoulder. "Yes, I am. It's a long ways on foot."

Mark chuckled. "Simon will be glad to see you. He has prayed for you many times."

"How old are you now, Mark?"

"Thirteen."

Mark had become a young man—and a fine one at that.

The bleating of the soon-to-be-sacrificed lambs filled the night air. Tiredness came over me as if Mark's words reached my aching legs.

We passed a dozen or more families before we arrived at Simon's tent.

Mark entered first. "See who I found."

Simon leaned forward on his blanket. "Daniel, is it really you?"

"Shalom," I said.

He stood and gave me a hearty welcome.

Simon said to Mark, "You did well. God will show you favor this Pesach."

Mark replied, "God will show us favor if we see Yeshua tomorrow."

Simon assured him. "We will. He's on the way from Jericho."

Mark rubbed his hands together. The tent did not keep out the cold night air. "I should be going. My father will be looking for me."

"Share the good news Daniel is here."

"I will," Mark replied.

The boy exited the tent and I listened as his footsteps faded away.

Simon smiled. "His father is nearby. We traveled here together."

"How did you know I was coming?"

Simon chuckled. "God told me."

I took a deep breath. Why didn't God speak to me like that?

Simon scooted closer and spoke in a hushed tone. "Daniel, everyone is searching for you."

"Everyone?"

"The Romans, that is. With your winnings, why did you steal the horses?"

I shook my head. "I didn't steal the horses. And I have no money. Only a laurel crown I hope to sell."

Simon leaned back. "You mean you squandered your winnings?"

"Someone stole my money."

Simon's eyes grew big. "So you lost your money and now want to get right with God."

I nodded.

"Where are the horses?"

"Cynisca took them with her to Galilee."

Simon waved his hand. "Good. I'm not speaking to a thief."

My hands felt clammy—what would happen if the Roman soldiers captured me?

Simon continued. "You know, there is only one person more sought after than you in Jerusalem."

"Who?"

"Yeshua."

I gazed at Simon and an awkward silence followed.

He changed the subject. "Let me spread out an extra blanket and share some bread."

"Thank you." My stomach had been rumbling for hours.

"Do you have a paschal sacrifice?" Simon asked.

"Not yet. I hope to purchase one tomorrow."

Simon waved his hand. "Outside the city gates are merchants where you can obtain a lamb—but you are more than welcome to share ours."

"You have one?"

"We gave ours to the priest—made Mark sad."

"Why?"

"We kept the little lamb for a week—long enough for him to bond with it."

"I see."

Simon added, "The sacrifice is God's way of forgiving us for our transgressions—the outward sign. Of course, Yeshua speaks of a change of the heart."

The whole idea of sacrificing an animal seemed barbaric. I ate some of the bread. The more I ate, the hungrier I felt. "I will head down there first thing in the morning."

Simon nodded. "I'm glad you returned. You seem more like the Daniel I remember from three years ago."

I drank the last bit of water from my empty skin. "Thank you for the food."

Simon talked about his family, his two daughters whom he wanted me to meet, and plans for the eight-day festival. "We will celebrate Pesach in Bethany. After Yeshua teaches at the temple, usually he comes back to Bethany for the evening meal. I want you to join us."

I nodded.

Simon continued to make idle conversation, giving me directions to his house, but my eyes were heavy and my mind wandered aimlessly, as if I was lost in a dream. I reluctantly leaned back on the blanket and fell asleep.

CHAPTER 4

The dream was too vivid not to be real. My mother stood on the porch in front of our apartment. Wringing her hands, she cried out, "Daniel?"

I awoke with a start. Where was I? Then I heard the familiar noises —dogs barking, the wind snaking across the valley, the smells—and remembered. I knew Jerusalem's whispers as well as I knew my name.

Why did I dream about my mother? Three years had passed since I had arrived in the seventh dimension. I prayed, "God, please bring me home after Pesach."

I didn't expect him to answer. Did my mother live here—in this parallel universe? Could I even find our apartment in the first century? I tossed and turned through the rest of the night until someone shook me in the morning.

"Wake up."

I turned over and rubbed my eyes. "What time is it?"

"Can I go with you to get a lamb?" Mark asked.

I pulled myself up. "Something smells good."

"Father and Simon are cooking. A man from the market gave them some fish."

I grinned. Fish for breakfast sounded good.

Mark asked again, "Can I go with you?"

"Maybe. Let's talk about it after the meal, all right?"

Mark nodded.

I rolled up my bed and walked outside. The temperature was cool but the sky was clear. Excitement filled the air. Children scurried about as weary travelers headed towards the Eastern Gate. I focused on the temple. Its pristine structure was stunning—much more imposing than the coliseum or pagan temples in Caesarea. Then I saw the Roman guards.

Simon pushed a bowl in front of me. "Have something to eat."

"Thank you." I took the food and propped my leg up on some rocks. Mark's father walked over and sat beside me. His appearance was as stunning as Simon's was.

Mark's father pointed at his face. "Yeshua healed me of leprosy also."

I took a few bites. "I wouldn't have believed it had I not seen both of you."

Mark added, "Yeshua healed the whole leper colony. You must meet him, Daniel."

"I've met him," I replied.

Surprised eyes peered back at me.

"Really, I have. Yeshua healed Nathan, the young boy I mentored in Galilee."

"So you know the Master?" Simon asked. "I didn't know you had met him."

"It was a while ago."

As I heard the bleating of lambs, I became distracted. Was this the festival when the Romans put Yeshua to death? I didn't want to hang around for that. I'd make my Paschal sacrifice, hopefully God would accept my offering, return me to 2015, and I'd promise to be a good Jew—even read the Torah every week.

If Shale and I could connect, life would be great. Medical school was still an option, but a distant one since I had lost my money.

Simon interrupted my musings. "I hope Yeshua comes to Jerusalem early enough to teach in the temple. Many pilgrims have never heard him."

I didn't want to get that close to the rabbi.

Simon lowered his voice, "Pontius Pilate has arrived from Caesarea." He waved his hand. "The Romans are everywhere. I hate their presence here. It causes too much strife among the Jews."

"Daniel said I might be able to go with him to purchase his lamb," Mark said.

I interrupted. "I need to run a few errands first. Suppose I pick you up this afternoon?"

Simon held up his mug. "Don't wait too long. The cost for an animal without blemish will increase."

I was glad Simon told me. I didn't know merchants would inflate the price as Pesach neared.

I stretched. "Thanks for the meal." I glanced at Mark. "I'll be back this afternoon."

Simon touched my shoulder and muttered in my ear. "Stay away from the Romans. They want you almost as much as they want Yeshua. Remember, you are an escaped slave. You kidnapped your owner's daughter, possibly murdered her, and stole two valuable racing horses —your owner's livelihood."

An unexpected cold chill made me shudder. "You didn't mention the murder charges last night."

Simon let go of me. "I was afraid if I asked, you would get upset. I was relieved when you told me you didn't steal the horses. I asked God when I went to sleep last night about the girl. He put me at ease that it wasn't true."

"I assure you, Simon, Cynisca is alive and well in Galilee. She is the daughter of the team owner I raced for, and I sent her away for her protection."

Simon nodded. "I understand."

I chided myself. How stupid I was to give up my freedom for the pursuit of money. "I'll be careful."

I glanced at Mark and his father. "Trust me, I don't want to be captured and put in a Roman prison."

SEVENTH DIMENSION - THE CASTLE, BOOK 3

"Crucifixion," Simon corrected me.

Mark added, "It's a terrible way to die—painful, inhumane, humiliating."

What did God want from me? I collected my bag. "I must be going."

Mark handed me my water jug. "I filled it up for you. Don't tarry."

"Thank you." I had almost forgotten it.

CHAPTER 5

As I picked my way down the Mount of Olives, I passed by families traveling with small children and an assortment of animals—lamb, sheep, and doves—all regulated by strict adherence to the Torah or Judaic law.

Temporary mikvehs, set up to accommodate the influx of visitors for Pesach, dotted the immediate area. A certain percentage of the water for the purification baths had to be from a natural source, like a lake. The cleansing baths ensured that temple visitors were ritually clean.

The beggars made me uncomfortable—there were so many. Late-arriving pilgrims unable to find space on the mountain would have to pitch their tents in the Kidron Valley or along the edge of the wilderness.

Tens of thousands of animals awaited slaughter. Humanity pressed in around me as families waited to receive approval of their animals by the priests. Others waited at the Eastern Gate to pay the temple tax. Everyone waited for something.

I was so nervous my hands shook. The excitement of being here made it hard to be patient. Only the Olympics might compare in extravagance and anticipation.

The temple towered above the city. Gold and marble decorated the sacred walls and massive columns surrounded the temple mount. How had Herod the Great, the ignoble, degenerate dastard that he was, been motivated to undertake such a massive building project? The construction took decades—almost unprecedented in any century.

A brisk wind blustered down the mountain, and I crossed my arms to keep warm. Doubts entered my mind. The Eastern Gate was the most convenient entrance and the closest to the temple. In this dimension, the apartment where we lived should be a short distance from the Upper City. Perhaps the other gates would be less crowded or not so heavily guarded.

The soldiers appeared to be paying close attention to young Jewish men traveling alone. I should have brought Mark along. They would be less likely to stop me.

My concern increased the longer I watched. The higher echelon of Rome knew me—many had clapped and cheered me on—Daniel, the greatest Jewish charioteer in the world.

Even if the Roman soldiers didn't recognize me, the laurel crown in my bag would give me away. I needed the crown to pay for the lamb, but I couldn't buy the lamb until I passed through the gate.

A Roman guard pilfered some clothes of an unfortunate victim. I hated myself for spending so much time in Caesarea, eating Roman food and enjoying their pagan lifestyle.

Could I pose as a woman? I still had the necklace. I ran my hand through my thick beard. I would need a scarf to cover my face. I flexed my muscles. Racing chariots had built me into a male specimen of enviable build. Did I really think I could fool anyone?

I remembered Hezekiah's tunnel. It connected to the Gihon Spring outside one of the gates—if I only knew which one. I stepped out of line and headed south, following the rocky wall—one of dozens. Practically every conquering country had built one. There were too many.

The spring was somewhere between the Kidron and Hinnom Valleys. If I found the entrance, I could walk through the tunnel—if there wasn't too much water.

I trudged along the wall searching for the towers. Discarded trash strewn along the pathway added to the stench. I walked up to an old man and tapped him on the shoulder. "Do you know where the Gihon Spring is?"

He stared at me blankly.

I shrugged. He probably didn't live here.

After several minutes, my persistence paid off. I found two large turrets built into the wall overlooking a small pool of water. Several decomposing walls next to the towers butted up to the spring at a steep angle. I didn't recognize the pool, even though I'd walked through Hezekiah's tunnel several times. On closer inspection, I saw water gushing into the spring. Was the opening large enough? It was smaller than I anticipated. The guard towers seemed abandoned.

I slid closer. Besides the heavy water flow, the dark cave entrance gave me the creeps. I climbed back up the slippery algae-covered side and cleared away the overgrown brush. There had to be another larger opening. From the archeological digs, a labyrinth of tunnels had been uncovered.

Suddenly my feet gave way and I fell through an abandoned shaft. My sandals smacked into the water. I went underneath and came up, but the darkness disoriented me. The impact knocked the bag off my shoulder.

After I slapped the water from my face, I noticed sunlight pouring through the collapsed shaft. Once my eyes adjusted, my sandals became visible. I quickly leaned over and snatched them before they floated away. A large exposed tree root had also snagged my bag. I tried to reach it but the current pushed me in the wrong direction.

I might be able to retrieve it from the other side. I lifted myself out of the water and climbed up on the ledge. Hunched over, I eased around the side so as not to hit the ceiling, but my bag was still out of reach. I'd have to get back in. From this side, though, the current would cooperate.

After several failed attempts, I held on to the large root and grabbed my bag. When I climbed out and opened it, the laurel crown gleaned. I checked to make sure I hadn't lost the Star of David. The water had washed off the dirt and the star shone in scintillating brilliance.

I hoped I had found Hezekiah's Tunnel and not some other tunnel. Perhaps God meant for my mishap to be my ritual cleansing.

I was uncomfortably cold, but once I made it out, I could dry off in the sun. I held up the crown for more illumination. The wide tunnel made it easy to travel and I could slush along in the water with my bare feet.

Discarded oil lamps filled the passage. People must have used the corridor in the recent past. After a vertical incline, the tunnel leveled out. Minutes later, straight ahead, sunlight pierced the darkness.

I bolted towards the opening. The pool of Siloam stretched out beneath the tunnel entrance. The massive size of the pool surprised me. Several men sat beside the calm waters. Many considered the pool to have healing powers.

No one noticed me but I stayed in the shadows a few more minutes. Although excited I had made it inside the city gates, I was cold.

I tucked the crown in my bag.

After making sure there weren't any Roman soldiers hanging around, I exited the tunnel and walked over to sit beside the pool. The ground was warm and felt good against my exposed skin. At the next wave, I hoped everyone else would be wet, too. I hated being the only one.

After a few minutes, someone nudged me from behind. I turned and saw an old man. He squinted in the sunlight and asked, "At the next wave, can you help me into the water?"

I studied the paraplegic—his deformity prevented him from walking. I leaned over and spoke softly, "I can wait a few minutes, but I must tend to my mother soon. If the waters aren't stirred up before I leave, perhaps when I return, I can help you."

The man nodded. "I have been this way my whole life."

His limbs were so disfigured they were probably beyond the healing powers of modern medicine.

"I'll come back and help you," I assured him, not knowing if I would. Why did I say that when I wasn't sure I could keep my promise?

The man smiled. "I believe you."

I sat for a few more minutes. "Wait for me," I told him.

He nodded.

The dream from the night before troubled me. I glanced up and asked God, "You will bring me back home to 2015, right? After Pesach?"

When the man saw I was really leaving, he looked sad. I clutched my bag containing the necklace of the girl on the train. Why was there so much suffering anyway? Did she survive? Would I ever know?

I passed the temple. In the Outer Court of the Gentiles, thousands of people milled about. Moneychangers were swamped—long lines wrapped around the columns. Souvenirs and trinkets brought in by merchants covered tables and display racks. The priests had done a superb job of ensuring there were plenty of animals for sale. Hundreds of lamb, sheep and doves packed the courtyard. I didn't see any temple guards but they wouldn't bother me anyway. The Romans would.

I turned south and headed towards the Jewish quarter—or what would be the Jewish Quarter in 2015. If this were a parallel universe, my mother would be here. I walked up and down the narrow alleyways.

The wealthy Upper City boasted of immaculate streets and properly maintained gardens. I imagined Pontius Pilate and his entourage by now settled into one of the nearby palaces. Herod Antipas was probably here—a half-Jew of the same ilk as Herod the Great.

I had almost given up when I came to a familiar residential area. I approached a row of yellowed, limestone dwellings—had I been here before? A woman stood in a doorway. Something about her caught my attention. Perhaps it was her protruding eyes or the familiar way she pulled back her dark brown hair.

She clasped her hands and flailed them in the air. When she saw me, she motioned vigorously for me to go away. Three years had passed since I'd seen my mother. Did she not recognize me? She mouthed "no." Was she angry because I had left?

I bolted towards the apartment but as soon as I came within earshot, she hurried inside.

"Mother, it's me, Daniel!"

CHAPTER 6

I leapt forwards two steps at a time. Seconds later, I reached the portico. Mother had disappeared inside and slammed the door. I flung it open but it was too dark to see through the opening.

Someone hit me and knocked me to the floor. Hands seized me underneath my arms and flipped me over. Someone kicked my bag and it slid out of reach.

"That's him," a voice said.

"Grab his bag. See how much money he has."

With the room spinning, I couldn't focus.

One of them shook the bag, spilling out the contents. The crown and necklace glistened in the sunlight pouring through the door.

Mother gasped.

Romans—I should have known better. Of course, they would be searching for me at my mother's house.

The older soldier stomped on the empty bag.

The younger one kicked me in the side and pain shot up my back. Shouting Latin vulgarities mixed with poor Hebrew, he asked, "What did you do with your winnings?"

I groaned, "Someone stole them."

I glanced at my distraught mother.

"All of it?"

I didn't respond.

"Strip him," the older soldier said.

"Get up," his partner demanded.

I stood as told, despite my pain.

"Remove your clothes."

My mother averted her eyes.

I took off my outer robe and threw it at the one in charge. He shook it and searched for hidden pockets. Grimacing, he turned his nose away. "He peed on himself."

The younger guard smirked.

The soldier slammed me in the face with the damp cloak. "You pig." He turned to his partner. "He doesn't have anything. Probably squandered his winnings."

"Or hid them somewhere," the minion replied.

I quickly slipped on the damp robe. The irony of the mikveh purification didn't escape me, but my humiliation lingered.

The superior officer shrugged. "Maybe we can pawn the crown." He reached over to pick it up. When his fingers touched the laurel leaves, he jerked his hand away.

"What's wrong?" the younger guard asked.

The officer splayed out his blistered fingers. "The crown burned me."

I silently thanked God for its magical qualities.

The minion said, "They told us to bring him in alive. They didn't say anything about his possessions."

The officer in charge agreed. "Let him keep his crown—a consolation prize."

I snatched the crown and flung the necklace at my mother.

The guards tied my wrists behind my back and shoved me towards the door.

"I'll be back," I promised as they pushed me outside. I'd told my mother and sister I would stay alert and awaken them if anything happened—and I left. Was this God's rendering of justice?

CHAPTER 7

The soldiers led me past the temple through the crowded streets of the Upper City. The gawking by lowlights paled in humiliation to the near stripping in front of my mother. Once I received the worst dishonor, degrees of degradation mattered little.

"Is the cell ready at the Antonia Fortress?" the minion asked.

The officer in charge smirked. "If not, we'll throw him in with Barabbas."

Who was Barabbas? I recognized the name, but I couldn't remember why. Familiar names usually meant ill repute in the first century.

With a spear pointed at my back, the soldiers kept me within arm's reach. The Upper City boasted of extravagant piety—the Sadducees, with their aristocratic and priestly wealth, lacked for nothing.

We trudged past opulent government buildings rarely used except during festivals. Pontius Pilate came only when it was required for official duties. The governance by the temple vanguard the rest of the time was tenuous. Several officials had overseen the affairs of Palestine since the Romans seized power following the Hasmonean revolt. Most didn't last a year.

"Pontius Pilate has arrived from Caesarea," the officer said. "Plenty of rabble-rousers to keep him busy, including this one."

His cohort chuckled. "I bet Pilate will send this one to the salt mines—much too physically endowed to crucify him."

The superior replied, "He's got plenty of men waiting in the dungeon for crucifixion. One more won't make any difference."

I cringed.

We passed the Hasmonean palace and continued along the Western Wall. Oglers eyed me with too much interest. The heavy chains chafed my wrists. We passed underneath the bridge leading down from the temple to the portico. Dozens of Roman soldiers, stationed every few feet along the walls, stood guard.

The clanging of the guards' shields was unlike any sounds in the twenty-first century. I wanted to hide in a cave—better yet, go back to my own world. I was not guilty of anything except running away. Technically, I wasn't a slave, but try convincing a Roman when he thinks you stole his horses and kidnapped his daughter.

The guards shoved me towards the steps. The Antonia Fortress stood high above the temple and the climb was steep. With my hands in chains behind me, I leaned forward to keep my balance.

When we reached the platform, more Roman garrisons filled the courtyard. The whole area contrasted sharply with 2015.

My memory of the future reminded me that the Dome of the Rock occupied this rocky outcropping. The Arabs forbid Jews access to the sacred ground. In my ancient reality, watchful eyes stationed at the fortress guarded the whole breadth of the temple below.

Another Roman guard approached. The two soldiers conversed in Latin. Having spent so much time in Caesarea, I understood the conversation.

"Take him to the holding cell."

We entered through the gate on the northwest side. One of the soldiers grabbed a torch and led the way through a maze of corridors. We came to some steps that disappeared into a dark hole.

The creepy dungeon contained several grated cells. Most of the pens held one or two prisoners. They took me to the empty block. The prisoners rattled the doors of their cages and tried to reach me with their hands. I felt like a toy for hardened criminals, a sheep among wolves. The clanging echoed off the cold rock walls.

The lead guard unlocked the gate and shoved me in. "Be happy we aren't putting you in stocks like the others. Try to escape and we will."

"All right." The chains on my hands were enough.

The guards locked the door and trudged off. Their laughter as they climbed the stairs stoked my anger. The sudden reality of being behind bars hit me like an exploding bomb.

The prisoner in the next cellblock banged on the gate. I ignored him. He banged louder.

To make him stop, I finally asked, "What's your name?"

"Yeshua bar Abba, known by my friends as Barabbas."

The same name the soldiers mentioned earlier. I couldn't make out the man's features.

"And yours?" Barabbas asked.

"Daniel, son of Avid, from Jerusalem," I replied. "Yours is Barabbas?" I repeated.

"Yes."

My association with the name returned. The Romans released Barabbas at the time of Yeshua's crucifixion. What lousy luck on my part. I did not want to be here when that took place.

The man lowered his voice. "What did the Romans get you for?"

"I'm a runaway slave. Stole some horses and kidnapped a girl. So they think."

The man replied, "Got to be more than that. What else did you do?"

"I didn't even do that," I corrected him. I inspected the gate. "I suppose they think I might have killed her. I was a gladiator, a charioteer."

"Daniel, the famous Jewish charioteer?"

"Yes."

"I thought he died in his last race."

"No. Only injured." I rubbed my eyes, suddenly remembering I no longer had contacts.

Barabbas shook the bars on the gate. The sound was loud and annoying. I wished he would stop.

"Listen," the man said. "We can send these bums back to Rome. I have dozens of followers waiting for my release. Freedom fighters. Join me and we can overthrow them. As Jews, we need to band together. We can defeat the Romans. Will you join us?"

Rome imprisoned Barabbas because he was a threat to Rome. Pontius Pilate would release him on Pesach. That was less than a week away. Could he help me to escape?

"I'll think about it."

The criminal shook the gate again.

"Barabbas, can you stop the racket?" someone hollered from an adjoining cell. "I'm sleeping."

"Gestas, it's the middle of the day. There is no time to sleep here," Barabbas retorted.

The man responded tersely. "Barabbas, you are going nowhere. Accept your fate. You're a dead man."

The two argued back and forth. Others added a word or two. I sat and listened, too disturbed to care. The cave dampness clung to my wet clothing. What did I do to deserve this?

If only I could get the chains off. While the others argued, I tried to slip my hands out of them. After a while, the chains chafed my wrists so much it hurt to keep trying.

I moved the bag around and reached inside to touch the crown. "God, please release these chains." I shut my eyes and blocked out the other voices.

Clasping the crown, again, I cried out to God, "Please set me free."

Immediately, the chains fell off my hands and onto the dungeon floor. I stared—shocked. I had never seen God answer my prayer like that. Or perhaps I never took the time to notice all the ways he helped me each day.

A few hours passed and I saw no one. Hunger pangs filled my stomach. "Barabbas, do they bring us food?" I asked.

"When they remember," he replied.

No one came and I grew faint with hunger. I didn't want to lie down on the foul-smelling floor. Without sunlight, I couldn't tell if it was day or night.

At last, the door opened above the steps.

The prisoners shook the gates crying out for food.

I put my hands behind me, pretending they were still in chains. I flinched. The crown lay on top of the bag. I forgot to put it in the bag. The visitor tapped the cells as he walked by and the subdued light revealed desperate hands clamoring for food.

The guard did not have anything to give us. He stopped in front of my cell. The man wore the typical Roman garb. His hollow eyes looked drugged.

He tapped the cell gate with a spear. "Daniel, son of Aviv, I've come to set you free."

I approached the metal door and studied the man.

The guard said, "You don't belong here. A mistake was made."

"Oh," I replied.

"You didn't steal the horses. The girl took them with her to Galilee."

My heart thumped wildly. Who was this man? How did he know?

The torch flickered and eerie shadows bounced off the walls. The guard showed me the keys in his hand. "All you have to do is slip the crown to me and I will set you free."

Did I value the crown more than my freedom? Did God send this man here to set me free?

Barabbas shook his cell gate. "Free me instead. I've been here longer than he has." Other prisoners yanked on theirs. One rasped pathetically, "I need my water refilled. I've had none today."

The visitor ignored all the rest.

"Open the gate first," I demanded.

He refused.

I studied the visitor's eyes. Something about his eyes bothered me.

"I can't give you the crown," I said at last. "It would burn you."

The guard's face turned a ghastly red and goose bumps crept up my back. Who was this man?

He turned and walked away, passing the other cellblocks to the stairs. Prisoners thrust their hands towards him. "Bread," they cried out.

The visitor slammed the door. For a brief moment, silence followed.

CHAPTER 8

Barabbas rattled the prison cell. Through the narrow wrought-iron slits, even in the dim light from a horned oil lamp near the stairs, his eyes blazed. I did not understand God—why he would allow Pontius Pilate to release this rabble-rouser on Pesach and send a kind rabbi to the stake.

I wanted to read Barabbas's mind, the gift God had given me in this dimension, but I didn't want to listen to his intense hostility. I had enough of my own contempt towards the Romans.

"Who was that woman? Barabbas asked. "Women don't visit prisoners here."

"What?"

Barabbas cursed me. "You heard me. Was she your concubine?"

Another prisoner exclaimed, "The man is a tax collector. Daniel must be in here for unpaid debts."

"Gestas, you think everybody is a tax collector," Barabbas retorted.

Another cage rattled and a third voice rasped, "No, the prisoner is a spy. The visitor was his informant."

Arguing ensued. Whatever the visitor's purpose, he had stirred up discord. Each prisoner saw someone different.

I walked over to see who was arguing and accidentally hit the crown against the bars. The whole gate sparked, as if someone had put something metal in a microwave oven. I jerked the crown away fearing I had damaged it. The prisoners gasped.

I touched the leaves—what kind of crown was it? The guard was a demon—no one could know the information he knew unless he was supernatural.

"Who are you?" Barabbas asked, enunciating the "who."

"He's a prophet," a prisoner exclaimed.

I ignored them. Where did the young girl say she got the crown? I forgot.

Barabbas continued with his scheming. "I have an army of followers who want to overthrow the Romans. With your power, we can do it. Join us."

Another prisoner, peering across the hallway, said, "I tell you, he's a spy."

Barabbas rattled the gate again. "Shut up, Gestas."

I held up the crown and touched the gate again, but nothing happened this time. Even the leaves were dark. Disheartened, I leaned against the cold wall. Bickering continued.

I examined the edges of the cave. Tally marks etched by a former prisoner impressed me. I counted them. Whoever made them must have been here a week, filling up the hours by carving the days in the bedrock. Being stuck in this cold pit that long could send even a sane man over the edge; yet, I imagined a full day had already passed.

I turned the crown over. Suddenly, a crimson red laser bolt shot out from the leaves and hit the tally marks on the wall. The lines turned into molten rock and joined into a glowing circle that ebbed and flowed. The crown guided my hand, pulling the glowing halo towards the gate. The circle wrapped itself around the bars and pulled them apart. Within seconds, a gaping hole had opened up through which I could crawl.

One of the prisoners whistled.

"The man is one of them, a follower of Yeshua."

"Shut up, Dysmas," Barabbas snapped.

The burning bars cooled slowly.

"Get us out of here," Barabbas demanded.

I put the crown in my bag and crawled through the hole. The ghost-like whites of the prisoners' eyes shone through the prison gates.

"Barabbas, you'll be set free," I said.

The revolutionary clenched his teeth. "How do you know?"

"What about me?" another one asked.

I shook my head. "I don't know about the rest of you. I must go. Tell the guards I left for Caesarea—we'll send them on a nice, long detour."

"Remember me," Barabbas demanded.

I wanted to tell him the whole world would remember him for the wrong reasons. I glanced around looking for an alternate escape route.

"He's one of Yeshua's followers," a prisoner said for the third or fourth time.

"I'm not one of his followers. I am a Jew," I corrected.

"So is he and his followers," the man said.

"They are different from me," I insisted, although I didn't know how. I didn't know who Yeshua was, other than a Jewish rabbi who performed miracles.

I glanced at each of the prisoners. Which one of you was thirsty?"

"Me," the man said.

I pulled my water jug out and handed it to him. "Take a sip. Hurry."

Barabbas rolled his eyes. "You'll give a man water, but you won't rescue us?"

The man handed the jug back to me. "Yeshua gives water to the thirsty."

Barabbas rattled the gate. "You and Yeshua. Get over him, Dysmas. That sage hasn't done anything for you."

I dismissed the comparison. There had to be a way out. There was always more than one entrance and exit to a building.

The historian Josephus had written about a hidden passageway from the Antonia Fortress to the temple. If I could find it, I could avoid the thousands of Roman guards patrolling the mount and streets above us.

CHAPTER 9

I scrambled away from the prison cell into complete darkness—so dark I became disoriented. How could I find a hidden tunnel without any light?

Running the tips of my fingers along the walls, I searched. Each indentation turned into a dead end. Discouragement led to doubt. Why would God deliver me from the prison cell and then leave me stranded here? I couldn't see anything in this impenetrable darkness.

I pulled out the crown and shook it, turned it over, rubbed the leafs —tried everything. Nothing happened.

With each passing moment, my muscles tightened. How much time did I have? The jealousy of the prisoners had ramped up into a near riot. The loud clanging as they banged on the cell gates continued. I rechecked the walls. How many dead end tunnels could there be? Perhaps there was value to their rants. The clamoring gave me a sense of location in the darkness.

Suddenly, I stumbled on an uneven drop and slammed against the wall. To my surprise, the wall moved. I leaned on it. Could this be the hidden passage? I needed light. Again, I tried to force the crown to do something—anything. What made the leaves come to life, so to speak, before—in the other tunnel? What made the crown emit the laser or spark when I accidentally brushed it against the metal gate? What was the trick?

A foul-smelling musk filled the tunnel and turned my stomach. Something was crawling on my sandals.

I cried out to God, "Please help me." Nothing magical happened except my heart pounded harder. This was not what I had expected. I went further into the tunnel. The numerous passageways reminded me of an ant farm. Why would there be so many?

I brushed against the cave wall and felt moisture. Water was a good sign. I ran my fingers along the wall. The deeper I went, the more wet the limestone became. I started to hyperventilate and struggled to catch my breath. A few leafs lit up. I had a tiny bit of light. What made them do that?

I skimmed the crown along one side of the cave and then the other. The light was still too dim. I leaned over and brushed the crown along my feet. Snakes! I had discovered Satan's lair.

Pretend they don't exist. Ignore them. Don't step on them. I walked a few meters. The tunnel narrowed. I heard water dripping. I walked a little further. A drop plunked me on my head.

I hoped my hunch was right. The temple needed water for the sacrifices. The Gihon Spring flowed into the temple from Hezekiah's tunnel. I knew of no other water source inside the city walls. My knees knocked. I didn't think I could keep going. Snakes slithered all around under my feet.

More tunnels intersected. The Muslims allowed no archeological work under the Dome of the Rock. No one knew anything about these tunnels—except for their experts, and they weren't sharing that information with the Jews. More water droplets fell from the ceiling. More laurel leaves shone. It dawned on me. The leaves needed water.

If only I had more. I flailed my hands about feeling for water droplets. I found a drip spot and held the crown underneath it. Another droplet fell, but it was too slow. I spit on the leaves. The crown sprang to life in a bright greenish hue.

A snake slithered up my leg. I slapped it away. "Get off me!"

I spit on the laurel leaves until my mouth had no more saliva. The light spread. I lowered the crown. The snakes hated the light. I brandished the crown back and forth.

"Go away!" Soon the snakes slithered into the darkness.

I relaxed a little and kept moving. The droplets increased. The temple must be directly ahead or above me. I came to a rickety wooden ladder. I held my breath as I climbed the first three steps. It appeared to be sturdy enough. I went up a couple of meters. Surface light filtered through the cracks.

Once I reached the last rung, I reached out to open the facing door. Rotten wood fell away and the door moved reluctantly. I tugged some more and jarred it loose. It rolled backwards. I covered my eyes to the blinding light and waited for them to adjust. Indistinct voices came through the open hole.

I crawled up on the platform and stepped outside the door. A courtyard opened up in front of me. Thousands of people covered the temple mount. The door I came through blended in so well with the wall, no one could have imagined a hidden tunnel to the Antonia Fortress behind it. I stepped out of the double column portico. Anonymity had become my gift from God—for the moment.

CHAPTER 10

In the afternoon sunlight, the temple sparkled in shades of white and gold. The large crowds created a celebratory and festive atmosphere despite the presence of the Roman soldiers. The elite peacekeepers evoked the familiar feeling—big brother was watching. Their regiments at the city gates, the temple, the Antonia Fortress, the streets, and countryside served as a constant reminder—the Romans had conquered them.

Nevertheless, I strolled through the courtyard glad to be free. It would take some time before the soldiers discovered I had escaped.

Multiple stoas filled the inner and outer courtyards. Double rows of tall white columns enclosed the cloisters. Four balusters surrounded the entrance. The outer wall around the temple consisted of huge stone blocks stacked to perfection one on top of the other. The precision was remarkable.

Rows of tables covered with enticing trinkets cluttered the temple entrance. Hundreds of caged, smelly animals in the outer courtyard added to the temple mystique. The temple priests ran the sheep mill to provide unblemished animals for sacrifice.

The temple bankers at the entrance converted foreign coins into the acceptable currency of the temple—an image-graven Tyrian coin containing a higher silver content.

While I wasn't an expert in fiscal affairs, this seemed like a conflict of interest. Nevertheless, Simon had recommended I buy my animal here. He said the priests would often find something wrong with sheep purchased from other venders.

The moneychangers were also part of the priestly aristocracy—a convenient way to keep the highly lucrative enterprise all in the family —at the lower and middle class's expense.

How did they build the temple and temple mount without modern technology? The grandeur of the complex spoke of the richness of Jewish culture. Thousands died in 70 A.D. when Titus burned the temple. The Romans plundered the countryside and hauled away millions in gold and silver. The Jews never recovered until 1948, condemned to spend the next two thousand years as sojourners without a country and persecuted by gentile nations.

I put aside the depressing thoughts. Of course, no one here knew the dismal future because no one here knew the future—except me.

The bleating of lambs pulled me back to reality. As I ambled along the stone mosaic walkway, I came to the soreg, a sort of boundary that Gentiles were not allowed to enter. A sign was posted in Latin, Greek, and Hebrew, "No foreigner may pass within the lattice and wall around the sanctuary. Whoever is caught, the guilt for the death which will follow will be his own."

Now I knew where I could hide from the Romans. Gentiles would be sentenced to death if they trespassed beyond the wall, including Roman soldiers and impure Jews.

Next to this area was a cloister in the courtyard known as the Court of the Women. I entered cautiously. An attractive young maiden smiled. I acknowledged her but walked away so as not to appear flirtatious. The Women's Court was an entryway to the deeper part of the temple.

Large circular steps led to the next gateway. Each level came nearer to the Holy of Holies. In the cloister above the Women's Court stood the Court of Israel. Only male Jewish laity and priests could pass through this door. Temple discussion by Jewish men filled the court-yard. I peeked into the cloister next to it where priests were performing temple functions.

Suddenly, hurried footsteps and thunderous excitement came from the Court of the Gentiles. I stopped my exploring to return to the outer court. People were pouring out of the temple entrance.

I stopped a young woman. "What's happening?"

Her eyes latched on mine. I recognized them, eyes that had sought me out to give me a New Testament two thousand years into the future —or her counterpart.

"Lilly?"

"You remember me," Lilly said, surprised.

I grinned. She wasn't Jewish. "Why are you here?"

Her eyes glistened. "Today the prophecy is fulfilled."

"What prophecy?"

She pointed to the Mount of Olives.

In the distance sat a man on a donkey. "Yeshua?"

"Yes, Lilly said. "The king comes riding on a donkey."

She smiled and raced off.

Yeshua's followers had increased since the last time I saw him a year and a half ago.

Singing erupted from the crowds outside the walled city. "Baruch haba b'shem Adonai. Blessed is he who comes in the name of the Lord."

Many waved palm branches. I was mesmerized at such extraordinary worship. As much as I had tried to minimize his ministry, I had seen him touch the people, heal the sick, and bring hope, even under the heavy yoke of Rome. Who was this eccentric holy man?

The people arrived from the streets, the valley, the mountain, and the wilderness. A procession formed snaking from the temple entrance through the Kidron Valley. The line extended up the slopes of the Mount of Olives.

I shook my head at the mass hysteria. Yeshua was more than a rabbi to the masses. He had become a deliverer from the Romans.

Several temple priests hurried through the Kidron Valley and cut through the long procession. I raced out of the temple to follow them. An imminent clash seemed unavoidable. The singing stopped when the temple vanguard appeared.

A few minutes later, one of the priests addressed Yeshua. "Teacher, rebuke your followers for saying things like that."

Yeshua replied, "If they kept quiet, the stones along the road would cry out."

The rebuffed temple leaders stepped back to allow Yeshua's passage. No doubt they feared a riot if they continued to block him. One held up a fist. Another crossed his arms in a simmering rage. But the crowds ignored the religious aristocracy and followed their king down the mountain and into the valley.

Why would the rabbi take such risks? These were the priests he rebuffed, the council. Was he that foolish?

Sobs came from the rabbi. He wept unashamedly. "For the days are coming upon you when your enemies will set up a barricade around you, encircle, you, hem you in on every side, and dash you to the ground, you and your children within your walls, leaving not one stone standing on another—and all because you did not recognize your opportunity when God offered it!"

How could Yeshua know this? Josephus had written of the fiery inferno when Titus destroyed the temple. The Romans had built the ramparts against the Antonia Fortress to provide a way to break into the temple.

The soldiers meticulously removed each boulder and threw them over the wall one by one to steal the gold that melted between the stone slabs. Thousands had died, including young children.

Was the rabbi a prophet of God?

I ran back to the Western Gate where the council waited. Neither the Pharisees nor Sadducees were celebrating. Their sullen faces betrayed deep-seated animosity.

As Yeshua approached, the Roman guards in their shining armor and shields stood at attention. Tension increased with each passing moment. Many of the rabbi's followers had placed their garments and palm branches on the ground in front of the Western Gate and at the temple court entrance.

The singing resumed as Yeshua entered the complex. "Hosanna to the Son of David—blessed is he who comes in the name of the Lord!"

The guards stood stoic, hundreds of them.

The rabbi's followers thrust their hands into the air in gleeful worship.

A voice called to me. "Daniel!"

It sounded like Mark. I hurried across to the other side. From here, I saw hundreds of pilgrims in the Kidron Valley and along the slopes of the Mount of Olives. The singing drifted above the temple. Even the bleating of the animals added to the holy festivities.

Someone touched me on the shoulder. "Daniel, I'm so glad you're here."

It was Mark.

"It's good to see you also."

His lips moved but I could only make out a few words in the din.

"What? I can't hear you."

His face tightened. "Why didn't you come get me yesterday to purchase your lamb?"

I sighed. "The Romans arrested me and put me in prison at the Antonia."

Mark's eyes grew wide. "How is it you are here?"

"I escaped."

"You must be more careful."

"You are wise, Mark. I was fortunate this time. Later today, I will purchase my sacrificial animal."

Mark nodded.

The singing lasted until Yeshua dismounted from the donkey. The temple leaders had left the area, perhaps hoping their abrupt departure would influence the crowds. It didn't. The Roman soldiers stood waiting. No one dared to do anything that might incite the masses to outright rioting.

Mark urged me, "Let's follow him."

I shook my head. "You'll never get near him. It's too crowded."

Mark pleaded. "Come with me, please."

I relented. The man of contrasts disturbed me. Beloved by the commoners and hated by the leaders, I wasn't sure who was right about the rabbi.

The deafening crowds grew. "Do you think he will teach today?" several asked.

The rabbi touched everyone who reached out to him, especially the children. He held some in his arms. His disciples, swallowed up in the excitement, never left his side.

Yeshua wielded so much power it was hard not to admire him, but his simple ways did not seem fitting for a king. He was too ordinary. Nothing impressed me about him physically. He was neither athletic nor handsome. Still, something different about him caught my attention.

I had tried to read his mind a year ago when he brought the young girl back to life, but something prevented me from doing so and knocked me to the ground. And his words about the destruction of the temple in 70 A.D. were too close to the writings of Josephus to be a coincidence. How could he know what happened if he wasn't a prophet of God?

The religious leaders glared at the rabbi and his enraptured followers. The powerful elite appeared quite impressive in their exquisite robes—a concession allowed by Rome for the Jewish festival, but their jealousy spoke louder. Despite the religious authority graciously delegated to the council by the emperor, the crowds cared nothing about the pious temple priests right now—a fact that didn't go unnoticed by council members.

The rest of us wore muted clothing, including Yeshua.

I rubbed my eyes and pleaded, "No, God."

I heard Mark's voice. "Are you all right?"

I nodded.

Uncertainly crossed Mark's face. He didn't understand my conflicted feelings.

Cheerfully, as if to yank me out of my musings, Mark said, "Yeshua healed my father of leprosy. He is the son of David."

"Yes, I remember your father in the leper colony," I reminded him.

We watched for a few more minutes. I reached over and wrapped my arm around Mark's shoulder. "I need to purchase my lamb. Now is a good time, while the Roman guards are busy here." He didn't know I still needed to hide from them.

Mark nodded but didn't move. "I will be close by."

I understood his reluctance to join me. He wanted to be near Yeshua.

I retreated towards the entryway. People, animals, and merchants filled every nook and cranny, making it difficult to navigate. Money clanged nonstop into the containers on the tables. The temple aristocracy was like the stock exchange, the Court, and the Vatican, all wrapped up into a wealthy conglomerate, largely supported by the poor and middle classes.

CHAPTER 11

I sat on a nearby bench and listened to the lambs bleating. Soon they would be slaughtered. My thoughts meandered. God had withheld his divine judgment on the Jewish slaves in Egypt who had painted the lamb's blood on the doorposts. The angel of death passed over them and did not kill their first-born child.

If God did that miracle, why didn't he do others? Why didn't he save the Jews during the siege of Jerusalem and the destruction of the temple? Why did he allow six million Jews to die in the gas chambers in World War II?

A few feet away, a priest thumped his chest and thrust up his hands. I supposed God heard his prayers—if only he would hear mine. Those walking by dutifully acknowledged his holiness with a nod of the head.

Was he that holy? Did chest thumping grab God's attention better than my heart-felt prayers?

Clutching my bag, I strolled to a table where the aroma of freshly baked bread filled the air.

The merchant was sweeping his stall. "Shalom."

I returned the greeting.

"Do you need a lamb for Pesach?"

"Perhaps, but I was more interested in your bread."

SEVENTH DIMENSION - THE CASTLE, BOOK 3

"No yeast. It's perfect for the Seder." He continued sweeping. "Since Yeshua is here, we will be leaving."

A young girl sat behind the table stroking a wooden horse in her hand. "We want to hear him teach. Father promised if Yeshua came for Pesach, we could go listen."

I smiled at the young girl.

Her eyes grew wide and she jumped up. "Daniel, is it you?"

"Yes." I peered at the girl. "I remember you. I gave you the horse at the chariot race, and—you gave me the crown."

The girl giggled. "Yes."

I chuckled. "What a coincidence we meet again."

Quick footsteps approached. I turned.

"Father, Yeshua is teaching in the temple."

"Soon, we will leave, after our customer departs."

The boy glanced at me and blurted out, "Daniel, the great charioteer!"

I laughed.

He ran over to a box and pulled out an object. He held up the chariot. "Here's the gift you gave me."

"Daniel, the charioteer?" a Roman guard repeated as he walked towards us.

My heart raced—and I quipped in Latin, "Yes, I hear he was captured."

The guard appeared confused.

"Good riddance." I hoped my Latin sounded convincing.

I turned to the young boy and spoke in Aramaic, "I never got your names."

The kids noticed my diversion. The young girl said, "I'm Anneliese and he's John."

"Nice names," I remarked.

The young girl pointed to herself. "Mine means 'devoted to God' in Hebrew."

The Roman shrugged and walked away. My ruse had worked.

After he left, I opened my bag and showed Anneliese and John the crown they had given me almost a year earlier.

"You still have it," Anneliese gasped.

"It's a magical crown."

"It is?" the girl asked.

I replied, "Where did you get it?"

Anneliese's eyes grew large. "God gave it to me—to give to you."

What could she possibly mean. "He did?"

"When we met Yeshua, he gave the crown to me." Anneliese turned to her father. "Father, what was it Yeshua said?"

Her father replied, "Yeshua told us to go to Caesarea and give Daniel, the charioteer, the crown." The man focused on me. "He even said your name, 'Daniel, the charioteer.' That's the only reason we went to Caesarea. What Jew goes to Caesarea to enjoy chariot races?"

"Why didn't you give it to me when I met you at the gate?"

"We weren't sure it was you," Anneliese replied. "We needed to make sure."

I stared at the crown. Who did she believe Yeshua was?

Anneliese glanced at her father. "He said something else, didn't he, Father?"

The children's father cleared his throat. "Yes. Yeshua said someday you would give the crown back to him."

I choked on my words, "I—I would give it back. When?"

The father shook his head. "I don't know."

John interrupted our conversation, "Father, we must hurry. You promised."

"Yes, I did promise." The father eyed me with kindness. "Here. You take this bread."

"Are you sure?"

"I promised Anneliese and John we would go listen to Yeshua if he came to the temple. This is the last of my bread."

I scooped it up. "Thank you."

"By the way," the man said, "I never introduced myself. I'm Stephen. You're welcome to share the Seder with us."

"That's a generous offer. Thank you."

"Today is my last day in the courts to do business."

"I understand," I replied.

The father asked a nearby merchant to keep an eye on his property and turned to his children, pulling them close to his side. "Yeshua wanted you to have the crown. It doesn't surprise me it has magical powers."

I nodded.

"He healed my wife of a sickness. He is a miracle worker."

The boy shook his father's hand. "Can we go now?"

"Actually," Stephen added, and he lowered his voice, "I believe he is the Messiah."

I wasn't sure what to say back. "Shalom."

I watched as they weaved through the crowds and slipped the crown in my bag. If that was the case, I must not sell it.

CHAPTER 12

No sooner had the family left than one of the merchants waved me over to his table. Cages lined the back of his stall. "Buy one of my lambs. They are at a very reasonable price."

"My animals are perfect, without a single blemish," another seller shouted. "And I will match his price."

Soon a dozen businessmen were competing for my business. I shook my head. "I have no money." I scurried away from the bazaar area surprised by the aggressiveness of the merchants.

I was afraid to leave the temple because of the Roman soldiers. The temple provided an element of safety. The soldiers couldn't go beyond the Court of the Gentiles. As long as Yeshua was here, I could hide among the crowds.

Thousands of pilgrims filled the temple. Hundreds more continued to pour in through the overcrowded entrance. I mingled among the visitors in the Court of the Gentiles until I stumbled upon the rabbi teaching at Solomon's Porch. His voice reverberated off the white marble columns and stone block courtyard, enhanced by the late afternoon breeze.

As I listened, his words surprised me. They were stabbing, biting, not like those I had heard him say to others.

"Woe to you, scribes and Pharisees, you hypocrites. You pay your tithes but you haven't done that which is more important—to show judgment, mercy, and charity. You are like blind guides, straining gnats out of water but gorging on camels."

I searched the courtyard for the temple vanguard. Several stood out among the crowds in their ornate robes and tubular hats—probably the rare moment they would have preferred anonymity.

Gasps rose from the crowd, but Yeshua's tirade continued. The Pharisees and Sadducees glowered at the rabbi. He was not the timid and mild prophet I had made him out to be.

"Woe to you, scribes and Pharisees. You make the outside of the cup or the platter clean, but on the inside, the cup is full of trash. You blind leaders, first clean the inside of the cup and platter so the outside may be clean also."

Several of the priests leaning against the balusters scurried away. The crowds stared as if stupefied into silence. Who had the courage to address the temple leaders in such an insolent manner? No wonder the Pharisees and Sadducees hated him.

Yeshua continued his tongue-lashing despite the sulky glares of the remaining temple priests. I chuckled. If the temple vanguard wanted to listen, they had to be visible. Perhaps this was Yeshua's payback. The temple priests had harassed him since he began teaching three years earlier. The priests had flaunted their status at others' expense. Today they had met their match. While outwardly the temple aristocracy appeared respectable, I sensed deep-seated anger seething beneath their pious skin.

Yeshua wasn't finished. "Woe to you, scribes and Pharisees, you hypocrites. You are like whitewashed sepulchers that appear beautiful on the outside, but on the inside, you are full of dead men's bones."

More gasps spread through the crowd. More Pharisees and Sadducees stomped off.

Was Yeshua correct? Who was he to question the authority of those schooled in the Talmud and the Torah?

Yeshua condemnations continued unabated. The rabbi was either stupid or insane or correct in his assessment—and didn't care. I wanted to tell him to stop saying such incendiary things, but his accusations continued.

"I will send you prophets and wise men and teachers. You will kill some by crucifixion and whip others in your synagogues, chasing them from city to city. I assure you, the accumulated judgment of the centuries will break upon the heads of this very generation."

The crowd grumbled. One person exclaimed, "Who would ever do such a thing? We are the sons and daughters of Abraham."

Yeshua's face softened. He lifted his eyes to the temple as if in a personal confession of sorrow. "O Jerusalem, Jerusalem, who kills the prophets and stones those who are sent to you. How I have desired to gather your children together, even as a hen gathers her chickens under her wings."

Yeshua lifted his hands. "Your house is left unto you desolate." He bored into the eyes of the few temple personnel remaining. "You shall not see me from now on until you say, 'Blessed is he who comes in the name of the Lord.'"

Yeshua's spectacular words silenced everyone—including me. Only the bleating of the sheep filled the temple courtyard.

The rabbi stood and exited Solomon's porch, departing through the Eastern Gate.

Grumblings followed when he left. "What did he mean?" a woman asked.

A man shrugged. "I don't know. I hope he will explain tomorrow."

The disciples followed Yeshua, leaving the rest of us to question. I watched from the temple entrance as they passed through the Kidron Valley.

Hopelessness filled me. Even if I didn't believe he was the Son of God or the promised Messiah, I had great compassion for him as a human being. Maybe he was a prophet. Whoever he was, he gave the people hope.

What did he have to do with me? Why was I here? To change

history? I glanced up at the temple—if God occupied the Holy of Holies, why didn't he answer?

The crowds dissipated. The Roman guards seemed relieved to have averted another showdown. Some of the people walked towards the Court of the Women. I followed.

Thirteen containers designated for offerings, shaped like long trumpets, lined one of the walls. The clanging coins reverberated through the cloister as they fell into the boxes. The offerings continued uninterrupted for several minutes.

My head spun. The temple donations must have been huge. Most of those making an offering were poor. Did the Pharisees and Sadducees use the money to help those who needed it most? Yeshua's scathing words of the temple aristocracy still rang in my ears.

I edged closer to the circular stairs that led up to the Court of Israel. Aramaic filled my ears. I passed through the golden Nicanor Gate and into the Court of Israel.

One pilgrim was complaining to whoever would listen. "They rejected my lamb and now I have to buy another one."

"What's wrong with your sheep?"

The man palmed his hands upwards. "The priest said the animal has a limp, though I can't see any limp." He shook his head. "Now I must buy one from the high priest's stock."

Another man said, "I don't see why we have to purchase Tyrian shekels."

A third man interjected, "So the priests can make more money. Those coins can only be obtained from the moneychangers."

Their discussion continued. I turned my attention to a group of men further away, where angry voices disturbed the temple ambience. Their attire meant they were priests and members of the council. I drew closer to listen.

"We must find a way to trap him."

"Trap him with his own words? Annas, forget it. We've tried that."

"We need to arrest him and bring him in for questioning, but it has to be when his followers aren't around."

"He needs to be put to death," Annas insisted. "He's a threat to our power. The masses hang on every word he says."

"Where does he go at night?" another asked.

The priests gazed at one another. No one had an answer.

"If we could find out, put a spy on Yeshua and bring him in when the people are still asleep—"

"We need a volunteer."

The eyes of the holy men searched the cloister.

"We don't have much time," another said. "This has to be done before the start of Pesach."

"That's impossible."

A priest threw up his hands. "What do you suggest?"

Two men had separated themselves from the rest towards the back of the cloister. I slipped closer to listen.

The men were elderly members of the council, but they weren't dressed in priestly robes. They were probably Pharisees.

One of them ran his hand through his beard. "Once I asked the sage how I could be born again."

"What did he say to you, Nicodemus?

"Joseph, I've never shared this with another member of the council.

"You have my confidence."

Nicodemus touched his beard again. "He said that until a man is born again, he cannot see the kingdom of God."

Joseph palmed up his hands. "We need the kingdom of God now. How can we see it?"

Nicodemus glanced at the temple. "Ask God to reveal to us the truth."

Joseph raised his eyebrow. "I know the truth."

"How can you be sure what truth is?" Nicodemus asked.

"I've known Yeshua since he was young. He's the fulfillment of the Messianic prophecies."

Nicodemus snatched Joseph's hands. "Why don't you tell the high priest?"

Joseph shook his head. "I keep praying God will open his eyes, as he has opened yours and mine."

Nicodemus warned, "If they capture him, they'll kill him. We can't let that happen."

I dropped my head and turned away. If two members of the council couldn't change events, who could? Messiah or not, did he have to die? If time was an illusion, how many different pasts could exist? The futility of being stuck in the first century grieved me if I couldn't change it. What was God's purpose bringing me here? Surely, this wasn't God's appointed time—that couldn't be changed—unless Yeshua was who he claimed to be.

CHAPTER 13

I hung around the Court of Israel until everyone left. The night air was chillier than I anticipated, but I couldn't leave the temple. I closed my eyes. I had visited the model of the temple in Jerusalem on many school field trips. I tried to visualize it.

A large platform area with vaulted arches occupied the area underneath the Court of the Gentiles. The Jews used it for centuries as a storage dump. An opening existed on the Eastern Wall, but I didn't want to exit the temple complex to find it. Winding stairs descended to Solomon's Stables on the northern corner of the courtyard.

During the Crusades, the invaders housed their horses and camels on the large platform. Maybe I could spend the night down there and escape the biting wind.

I left the Court of Israel through the beautiful Nicanor Gate and walked down the curved stairs to the Court of the Women. A loud boom reverberated off the pillars. The court personnel had closed the massive gates to the temple for the night.

Continuing through the Court of the Gentiles, I breezed past several cloisters. Devoid of visitors, the platform seemed even larger. Several minutes later, I found the stairs. The accuracy of the model surprised me. Considering my precarious existence hiding from the Romans, I had much for which to be thankful.

As I descended into the bowels of the temple, darkness wrapped its cloak around me. I sprinkled some water from the jug onto the crown. Green neon light sprung forth from the leaves, but not as brightly as before. I sprinkled more water on the leaves.

A thorn pierced my finger. "Ouch!" I exclaimed, surprised. I had never felt a thorn on the crown. I stopped to wash off the blood from my water bottle. Was that an omen, a harbinger of the future? I hated not knowing.

The steep stairs continued several levels down. As I descended, the air became oppressively stagnant. When I reached the bottom, the platform felt abandoned—at least not in recent use. Row after row of vaulted arches supported by pillars rested on massive Herodian blocks. Even with the stale air, I preferred it to the biting wind up above. The light from the crown would make the darkness tolerable.

The arches and pillars continued in all directions. Here and there, discarded wooden boxes cluttered the platform. A sudden uneasiness made me uncomfortable. I changed my mind and started to go back up the stairs when a different kind of box startled me.

The container glowed in the dark. I held the crown up to see. Effervescent worms on the outside of the box gleamed—dozens of them. The sight of such ugly creatures made me squirm. What were they doing here?

I searched for a stick with which to flip them off the box. When I removed them, the worms became aggressive. I was careful not to touch them—perhaps they were poisonous. After getting the strange creatures off, I carried the bare wooden container to the stairs.

The box was light, weighing no more than a few pounds. After struggling to remove the warped wooden top, it snapped in two. My heart raced. I held the crown over the top and saw a scroll. Written across the front was the word "Daniel."

I lifted it out of the box and examined it. I tried to open it, but there was some kind of seal on it that I couldn't break. Strange.

My mother named me after the prophet Daniel who lived in

Babylon over five hundred years before the first century. Shale and I used to spend hours talking about mysteries like this. As long as they didn't concern Yeshua, anything was open to discussion. I missed not having her around now—to talk about what this scroll could be. Nothing was as it appeared in this century—which was frustratingly painful.

When I looked up, two eyes stared at me in the darkness. The green dots glowed too intensely to be human. Fear froze my legs, as if they were stuck in concrete. I put the scroll-like book into my bag but kept my eyes on the intruder. As the creature approached, his eyes grew larger. I eased up the stairs, not wanting to provoke him, but I missed a step and tripped. The crown skidded down the stairs.

As he drew nearer, the crown's light revealed he was a dog. I relaxed—but only a little. Gingerly, the dog picked up the crown and climbed the stairs. He plopped it on the step underneath my feet and scurried away.

I scooted down and clutched it. The dog lurched to the side, but his eyes stayed focused on me. I hesitated. He yelped and jumped forward. He must want me to follow him. A minute later, he brought me to a bed of old rags and blankets. Either he dragged everything here or someone provided the bedding for him.

He crouched down on the blankets and I scooted beside him. His warmth felt heavenly on my cold body. God had given me a blanket to sleep on and a warm dog beside me. I glanced up into the darkness and patted the dog on the head.

"Thank you."

CHAPTER 14

W hat sounded like thunderous applause awoke me. I struggled to remember where I was. I glanced around in the darkness looking for the dog. He must have left, and the light from the crown had faded. The platform vibrated ominously

I secured my bag. I needed a tiny shred of light—any light. The pounding continued. I groped like a blind man, shuffling my feet, so as not to run into the supporting pillars or low-level arches. At last, I found the stairs. The muffled cries of animals echoed down the stairwell.

I raced up the steep steps as the clamor increased. When I reached the temple courts, I discovered hundreds of animals were running through the Court of the Gentiles.

Doves circled overhead. Frightened lambs, some injured from the stampede, limped around in a stupor. Others had already escaped into the streets. Overturned merchant tables cluttered the entrance.

In the Royal Stoa, a man with a whip shouted, "How dare you turn my Father's house into a marketplace!"

I rushed over. Yeshua's disciples cowered nearby. Was it the rabbi? The man flailed the whip turning over more tables and chairs. Temple visitors had scattered. Many had fled into the women's court. Terrified eyes peered through the gate.

Temple priests approached. I hid underneath an overturned table and winced. More guards poured into the Court of the Gentiles.

Yeshua stood in the stoa as sweat poured down his face. His labored breathing and beet-red eyes blazed with enormous fury.

Singing drifted into the Court of the Gentiles from the women's court. Perhaps the Levites wanted to create a diversion. If Pontius Pilate had to restore order in the temple, the Romans could seize the power they had entrusted to the council.

Safely out of sight, I listened to the discordant commotion. Suddenly a couple of doves flew out from underneath my overturned table. The guards turned towards me. I panicked. How would I explain my covert presence?

One of them mumbled, "Only birds." They stopped abruptly.

I relaxed, but something disturbing made it temporary. Before I could blink, my eyesight turned gray. Again. I blinked. This couldn't be happening to me.

Yeshua ignored the approaching priests and bolted to the money-changer tables. He hurled the whip across the boxes and the containers flew through the air. Loose coins rolled around on the mosaic platform.

"You have turned my house into a den of thieves," he shouted.

The priests waited for him to stop.

The rabbi turned to face them, reluctantly.

One of the temple vanguard waved his hand at the overturned tables and freed animals. He asked, "What miraculous sign can you show us to prove your authority to do these things?"

Yeshua threw the whip down. "Destroy this temple, and I will raise it again in three days."

The priest rolled his eyes. "It has taken forty and six years to build this temple and you will raise it in three days?"

Yeshua remained silent.

The temple personnel left, shaking their heads. The tension lifted and the guards moved on. I was surprised they didn't press the issue further, but many of Yeshua's followers were watching.

I focused on the emblazoned rabbi as my eyesight returned. Color appeared on Yeshua's reddened face and spread to the rest of the temple. Could I be causing this? Was I going crazy? Uneasiness swept over me because there was so much I didn't understand.

I reached into my bag and pulled out the scroll to examine it in the sunlight. I still couldn't open it—like something supernatural had sealed it.

Time was ticking. How much longer did Yeshua have before the temple vanguard captured him?

CHAPTER 15

What did Yeshua mean by his strange comment, "Destroy this temple, and I will raise it again in three days?"

The platform covered the size of several soccer fields. The temple was nine stories tall. The Western Wall was almost sixty meters high. Yeshua was too intelligent to make fanciful statements. His words must have another meaning.

The merchants returned to collect the spilled coins, recapture the animals, and clean up. Many of the venders were taking down their tables. Apparently, they got Yeshua's message. The rabbi leaned against a pillar on Solomon's Porch. Some who had retreated into the Court of Women came back, including a few pompous temple leaders.

When the people had re-gathered, Yeshua went and sat before his audience.

I joined them.

The teacher studied his listeners and waited until everyone was ready. "A wealthy businessman bought some land and built a winery. Since the land was previously fallow, the prudent investor poured many shekels into the start-up business, setting up irrigation, constructing a protective wall around the acreage, and building a watchtower.

"After a while, the landowner needed help managing the joint venture, so he hired some farm hands. Soon he needed to take a trip out of the country.

"Unexpected delays kept him from returning for the fall harvest, so the absent owner sent his most trusted workers to the farm to collect his share of the profits.

"But the ungrateful tenants attacked the landowner's representatives. So the investor sent more workers, more than the first time, and the heartless tenants treated their boss's representatives the same way. Finally, the man sent his own son. 'They will treat my son as if he were me,' the landowner said.

"But when the workers saw the son, they said, 'This is the heir. Come, let's kill him and take his inheritance.'

"When the landowner returns, what will he do to those wicked tenants?"

Several from the crowd responded, "The businessman will bring those worthless wretches to an end and rent the farm out to others he can trust, who will give him his share of the profits."

Yeshua glowered at the temple priests. "Have you never read in the Scriptures, 'The stone the builders rejected has become the capstone'? The kingdom of God will be taken from you and given to a people who will produce fruit. He who falls on this stone will be broken to pieces, but he on whom it falls will be crushed."

The courtyard was silent except for the footsteps of priests leaving. An awkward moment followed while the rest contemplated the meaning of the story. After a while, one of the teachers of the law asked a question. "Of all the commandments, which is the most important?"

"The most important one," Yeshua replied, "is to love the Lord your God with all your heart, soul, mind, and strength. The second one is to love your neighbor as yourself. There is no commandment greater than these."

The listener smiled. "To love God with all your heart, understanding, and strength, and to love your neighbor as yourself, is more important than burnt offerings and sacrifices."

Yeshua replied, "You are not far from the kingdom of God."

No one else asked him any more questions.

By mid-afternoon, hundreds of people had crowded into Solomon's Porch. When I saw Simon in the crowd, I rushed over and touched his shoulder."

"Daniel," Simon exclaimed.

"Shalom."

"I'm glad you're here."

"Me, too," I agreed.

Simon motioned for me to sit. "You must come back with us to Bethany tonight. Yeshua is the guest of honor. Martha and Mary have been cooking all day. You can meet the rest of my family—including Lazarus. Yeshua raised him from the dead."

"Raised him from the dead?"

Simon chuckled. "That's what turned the council against Yeshua."

I whispered, "How could such a miracle upset the council?"

"When is the last time a priest raised someone from the dead?"

"They feel threatened by him, don't they?"

"Yes."

The person sitting next to us elbowed me. "Be quiet, I'm trying to listen to the Master."

"I want to come," I said softly.

Simon smiled, "Good."

Yeshua spoke for a while longer, but it was late and some people had already left. The rabbi walked over to the Court of the Women and returned. As he and his disciples were exiting the temple, I overheard someone say, "Look, Teacher. What massive buildings."

Yeshua waved his hand. "Do you see this building? Not one stone here will be left on top of another. Every one will be thrown down."

That was the second time he had referenced the destruction of the temple. How could he know? No one could know unless he was a prophet sent by God—or came from the future, like me.

A small crowd, including Yeshua's followers, exited the temple. Simon and I followed through the Kidron Valley. We stopped to rest on the Mount of Olives.

As we relaxed, one of Yeshua's followers asked, "What will be the signs of the end of the age?"

I sensed a long discourse.

Yeshua studied the questioner and glanced around at his captive audience. "Watch out that no one deceives you. Many will come in my name and lead many astray. When you hear of wars and collapsing governments and anarchy, don't be alarmed. Such things must happen, but the end is still to come. Countries will rise up in arms against one another, breaking treaties and making false promises. There will be earthquakes in remote areas, pestilences, and famines. These are the beginning of sorrows."

I pulled the scroll out of my bag and rubbed my finger along the seal, listening to the teacher's words. My mind raced. Could Yeshua open it?

The rabbi's closing remarks disturbed me. "False Messiahs and false prophets will appear and perform signs and miracles to deceive the believers—if that were possible. So be on your guard. I have told you everything ahead of time."

How many times in the last two thousand years had self-proclaimed Messiahs come along? Too many. I remembered Simon bar Kokhba from the second century, who founded a short-lived Jewish state before being defeated in the Second Jewish-Roman War.

More recently, Menachem Mendel Schneerson had many followers who claimed the rabbi was the Messiah—before he died in 1994. So much for Jewish Messiahs. Most scoffed at the idea—disappointed too many times.

Yeshua continued. "In the latter days, following overwhelming hardship and distress, the sun will be darkened. Fear will seize the world as the moon turns black. Stars will appear to fall from the sky. Indeed, all the heavenly bodies above will be shaken."

The teacher raised his hands. "Then all will see the Son of Man coming in the clouds with great power and glory. And he will send his angels and gather his elect from the four winds, from one end of the earth to the other."

Was Yeshua referring to himself or someone else? The Jews considered this passage a Messianic prophecy.

The rabbi continued. "Now learn this lesson from the fig tree." Yeshua pointed to a nearby tree. "As soon as its twigs become tender and its leaves emerge, you know that summer is near. When you see these things happening, be alert. The end is near—even right at the door. This generation will not pass away until all these things have taken place."

If the fig tree symbolized Israel, which every Jew knew it did, what did he mean, "this generation will not pass away until all these things have happened"?

I hid his words in my heart, but did it matter? The rabbi was a spectacular prophet but he couldn't be the Messiah. The Messiah would put everything under his feet. Yeshua couldn't even save himself. I knew he would soon die without ever fulfilling the Messianic dream—to bring peace to Israel.

I studied the amazing man—his presence, his intellect, his passion, and his love. He would have made a great Messiah—if only he had been the one.

CHAPTER 16

When we entered the home of Simon the Leper, a great entourage followed us. Swells of neighbors and friends arrived with more food.

Martha and Mary extended warm greetings. "Shalom, shalom."

We washed our feet with fresh, cool water set out for the occasion. Food and wine were plentiful. After having eaten only bread for a couple of days, the taste of honey, nuts, fruits and other delicacies thrilled me. The aroma from the kitchen reminded me of my mother's cooking.

My joy overflowed to see Simon surrounded by his loved ones, Yeshua, and the disciples. The leper's hideous scars and nubby fingers were no more. I doubted modern medicine could even heal someone so completely.

Those who wanted to get close to the rabbi crowded around him. The disciples left his side to mingle with the others. One of them approached me and introduced himself.

"Peace be with you, Daniel. I'm John, son of Zebedee, and a brother of James."

"Shalom," I replied. "Simon is an old friend. I used to help Doctor

Luke by bringing food and supplies to the leper colony—before Yeshua healed Simon and the others."

John smiled. "Yes, Simon told me about your kindness."

"Lazarus is coming," someone shouted. Many of the houseguests ran to the door.

The healed man entered the house amid much gusto and excitement. How many times in life did someone get to hug a man raised from the dead? The news had spread all the way to Jerusalem.

I remembered the hushed conspiracy inside the walls of the temple. "We must capture Yeshua," one Pharisee said, but no one knew how. As Simon had pointed out, the popularity of the sage incensed the temple leaders. If only I could warn Yeshua of what was about to happen.

I started to drift off when someone plopped down beside me.

"Daniel, wake up."

I opened my eyes. "Lilly."

She laughed. "Yes, it's me. You were invited?"

I nodded. "I knew Simon when he was a leper."

Lilly gazed at me.

I lowered my eyes, remembering Shale.

"Are you one of his disciples?" she asked.

"I don't think so," I replied.

Lilly shrugged. "What would it take for you to believe Yeshua is the promised Messiah?"

"You believe he's the Messiah?"

"I know he's the promised Messiah," Lilly said with deep conviction.

As we talked, a woman with a small jar entered the house. She scanned the crowded room. When she saw Yeshua, she hurried over to him before anyone could stop her. She knelt in front of the rabbi as he reclined at the table, eating with Simon and his friends. Letting down her hair, she wept openly.

Her almost scandalous actions caught everyone's attention. With trembling hands, she broke the alabaster jar and poured out the contents. A sweet aroma filled the room, mingled with the roasted lamb and cumin.

Everyone watched, but no one said a word.

Finally, one of Yeshua's disciples broke the awkward silence. "Why was this perfume not sold for three hundred denarii and given to the poor?"

"Leave her alone," Yeshua replied. "She has saved this perfume for the day of my burial."

The woman dried Yeshua's feet with her hair.

The teacher gazed at the disciple who had rebuked the woman. "You will always have the poor with you, but you will not always have me."

Did Yeshua know he was going to die? No one seemed disturbed by his comment. Did no one believe him?

I turned to Lilly. "What did he mean by the day of his burial?"

Lilly's eyes became watery. She whispered, "Mary's anointing him."

"I don't understand."

She slid closer to me. "Yeshua comes to a leper's house, allows a young woman to touch him, rebukes the Pharisees and Sadducees, and—frees my friend, a prostitute, from the men who used her"—Lilly clasped my hands—"do you know how many enemies he has? How long do you think he can live in this world among so many who hate him?"

"Enough to fill history books for two thousand years."

Confusion crossed Lilly's face but Yeshua's words deflected my comments when he added, "Wherever the good news is proclaimed around the world, what she has done will be told in her memory."

The only sound in the room was the woman weeping as she dried his feet with her hair.

The disciple who questioned her actions rolled his eyes.

I tapped on Lilly's arm. "Which disciple is that?"

She followed my gaze. "Judas. He's the treasurer, in charge of the money."

"Oh," I replied. "I guess that explains his concern."

Lilly leaned into me and whispered. "He's a thief."

"He is?"

Her eyes flashed.

I forced myself to suppress my anger. Another thief like the Naser brothers who stole my chariot racing winnings. I was afraid to ask anything else.

I wished I had the New Testament Lilly gave me in 2015—or her counterpart gave me. If only I could change history and prevent this good man from being murdered. Surely he must have many more good things to teach. Who knows what else he could have accomplished if only he'd lived a full life?

Yeshua spoke openly of his death, making it even harder to understand him. I took solace in the fact no one else seemed to understand the rabbi either.

CHAPTER 17

I couldn't remember how many times I had visited the fortress in my dream, but the high mountain, the citadel at the peak, and the floating, semi-transparent ball beside it never varied. I stared at the mysterious stone castle across the water. The only difference from my previous dreams is I didn't remember seeing water surrounding the castle.

I floated across the river and arrived at the castle's shore. I had no shoes, so I climbed the steep hill in my bare feet. After a while, I couldn't feel my toes. Snowflakes fell and I blew on my numbed, frost-bitten fingers. I tried to see the mountaintop, but clouds rolled in before I reached the top.

I entered the castle through the same wrought-iron gate. The familiar translucent ball remained stationary. Once inside the castle, the flickering torches on the walls provided only a scant bit of light. I held up my hands to thaw them out. As my fingers warmed, I noticed the pristine mosaic on the marble floor. Where had I seen the mountain? I couldn't remember

I checked the doors on both sides of the long corridor—locked, as always. I proceeded up the creaky stairs.

At the top, I unbolted the massive door. My father sat on a large wooden chair at the far end of the room. He appeared groggy from sleep—half laying down and half sitting up, but at least his hands were free, a small consolation after two years of seeing him in my dreams chained to the wall.

I ran over and hugged him—then collapsed in front of him on my knees. His tired eyes, pale skin, and sunken face revealed the stress of living in captivity.

"Father, I've missed you so much."

"You too, son."

We held each other until the familiar footsteps pounded on the creaky stairs.

I clasped his shoulder. "What is the name of this castle? I will come back and rescue you."

"Perlsea Castle—high up in the mountains of Nepal.

"Nepal," I exclaimed. "Who brought you here?"

"Go, before they see you. Don't lose the scrolls."

I ran and hid behind a window curtain. I lifted the curtain edge enough to peek out the corner. Two men entered. One was young and spry—the other man was older. He wore thick glasses and carried a brown paper bag. They walked over to the antique wooden chest I had hid behind previously.

The men spoke in an unfamiliar language as they opened and closed each drawer. A few minutes later, the men approached my father. I ducked my head back behind the curtain. Something smacked the table. "Food," the man said.

Then I heard coins clanging and rolling around on the table.

The older man spoke with a thick accent, making him hard to understand.

My father answered in Hebrew before switching to Arabic. "Only fools compromise for money. I can't be bought."

I peeked again.

The man frowned. "Sooner or later, you will tell us where the scrolls are." Again, he spoke in a language I didn't recognize, so how did I understand him?

"Never," my father replied.

We shall see," the man scowled. "Everyone has his price."

The younger man turned towards the window. I pulled my head back behind the curtain, but not quickly enough.

Footsteps came towards me. Seconds later, the man ripped the curtain away and icy-cold eyes stared at me.

I woke up hyperventilating.

The dream was too real. I wanted to rescue my father, but how could I? Where was the Perlsea Castle in Nepal? What was my father doing there anyway? And what scrolls—the one I found in the temple? Or was there another one?

I made a note of everything I saw and heard. Even though I had dreamed this before, I'd never gotten this far or remembered so many details.

Suddenly, a flash of recognition hit me. The mountain in the mosaic on the floor was Mount Everest. The castle must be somewhere near the mountain peak. We had gone to Kathmandu once on vacation—a popular destination for Israelis.

The only people who hung out around Mount Everest were mountain climbers and Sherpas. Wait—I remembered something else—the yeti tattooed on the arm of Nidal—the thief who stole my hard-earned charioteer earnings that I'd saved for three years.

The creature lived in the Himalayans. Few people had ever seen it. Many believed the animal was only a legend.

I seized my moneybag and pulled out the only scroll I had. Was this the scroll—but he said scrolls. I only had one. How did my father get them? He didn't deal in antiquities. He sold expensive cloths to travelers along the Silk Road between Israel and Syria.

Too many questions, but the possibility that my father was still alive in 2015 filled me with hope.

The police had searched in Syria, not in the Himalayas. I must get back to 2015, but how? Surely God would help me get back if I offered a sacrifice for him on Pesach.

I rolled out of my sleeping bag and tiptoed to the front door. I didn't want to disturb the others, but I needed fresh air. I was tempted to return to Jacob's Inn, my entry point to the first century.

I shook my head. I couldn't. Pesach would be starting soon. Jews couldn't travel that far on festival days. According to the Jewish calendar, there were two Shabbats this week—the regular one and the Feast of Unleavened Bread the day after. I'd have to wait.

I opened the door and walked outside. The sun had risen over the horizon. I sat beneath a fig tree that had no figs. A few minutes later, a shadowy figure emerged from Simon's house. He walked briskly towards the Mount of Olives. Should I read his mind to find out who he was?

CHAPTER 18

The mysterious figure's furtive movements—cloaked in black, and sticking to the shadows—alarmed me, so much I was afraid to read his mind. The icy eyes that caught me behind the window curtain in the castle in my dream still lingered. The chilly wind cut through me and goose bumps spread over my exposed skin.

The air shivered as if possessed and a supernatural heaviness seeped into my soul. Could evil touch even God?

A dove flapped close to the ground yanking me back to reality. After a while, the secretive traveler stopped. When he turned, I saw his face. It was Judas—the thief, as Lilly described him.

Why would he go to Jerusalem without the rest of the disciples? Yeshua and his followers always traveled together. I hugged my arms in front of me in a futile attempt to stay warm.

Every few seconds Judas stopped and listened. He appeared more edgy when he reached the Mount of Olives. He jerked his head from one side to the other. Then he descended from the Mount of Olives and hurried through the Kidron Valley. When he arrived at the Eastern Gate, he breezed through the entrance. The guards were not yet on duty. It was too early. I determined to keep following him—too curious to know where he was going.

Judas sped through the Eastern Gate and hurried towards the temple complex. When he reached the gate at the outer court, he stopped. I was the only one around. I slipped behind a baluster, but I couldn't see very well. I ran over and hid behind a closer column. The disciple stood still for several seconds. I grew impatient.

Suddenly his body became rigid. His head jerked up and his arms fell limp beside him. Did he know I was watching? I retreated behind the pillar, but I couldn't resist another glimpse, spellbound by his strange behavior. His glazed-over eyes flashed and a fork-like tongue fell out of his mouth. The sides of his tongue clung unnaturally to his lips. His arms stiffened as he stared straight at me.

I ducked behind the column, petrified. I waited a few seconds before peeking again. Judas had wrapped his arms around his torso. A black ink encircled him, tighter and tighter. The gaseous substance entered his skull and disappeared inside his body. Nausea overcame me as the world spun out of control. I leaned against the baluster to keep from falling.

When I recovered enough to see, Judas's appearance had returned to normal.

Had I imagined what I witnessed? Judas straightened his tunic, brushed his hair back, and smacked his face, as if smoothing out any tell-tell signs of the occult.

A wicked smile crossed his lips. I ducked behind the column. Grotesque images invaded my mind. It was as if something evil insisted I read Judas's thoughts. I tried to resist. I collapsed to my knees and covered my face with my hands.

I hadn't attempted to read anyone's mind in a while. Now I had no choice. A demonic madness had invaded Judas and threatened to overtake my sanity. Why would Yeshua allow anyone so evil to be his disciple?

I crouched frozen behind the pillar. Someone tapped me on the shoulder. I panicked, tried to get up, and fell.

"Are you all right?" the man asked.

I peered up at him. The man's clothing had blue fringes on the corners and he had a leather box tied to his forehead. I knew the box contained Scripture passages—even though I had never worn the tefillin.

"I'm fine," although I felt embarrassed.

The Pharisee studied me. "I saw you lingering the other night in the Court of Israel and listening to Yeshua in Solomon's Porch yesterday."

"There is much I don't understand about the teacher."

The council member bowed slightly.

I had forgotten which Pharisee he was. "What is your name, might I ask?"

The man tugged at his beard. "Nicodemus."

He was one of those at odds with the council concerning Yeshua. If only he knew what was about to happen.

"I need to go to a meeting," the Pharisee said.

"Thank you for your concern. I appreciate it."

He cocked his head. "Perhaps we can talk later."

I followed him at a distance to the Court of Israel. To my surprise, Judas was talking to some temple priests. Nicodemus joined his colleagues.

I listened.

"How much will you pay me to deliver Yeshua into your hands?" Judas asked.

"Wait here for a minute," one of the council members replied. The temple priests stepped away to confer. The court area was large, and I pretended to mind my own business.

I couldn't hear all their words and I doubted all the council members and temple vanguard were present, but those who heard Judas's offer spoke excitedly—except for Nicodemus. He shook his head.

The men returned, appearing quite pleased. My stomach churned. This was treachery.

A Pharisee handed Judas a bag. "Here are thirty pieces of silver. Do it quickly."

Judas snatched the moneybag and promptly exited the court,

brushing past me on the way out. No one said anything for a moment. Then several of the priests burst out laughing. "We should celebrate."

Another priest cautioned, "Let's wait and see if he delivers. Then we'll celebrate."

Nicodemus excused himself from the meeting, resignation written across his face.

"I must find Joseph," he whispered as he passed me.

I didn't know what to do—if I should return to Bethany or stay at the temple. I wanted to warn Yeshua of Judas's intentions. Perhaps if Yeshua stayed away from Jerusalem, he could still escape with his life.

I ran out of the courtyard, but when I reached the Eastern Gate, dozens of Roman soldiers guarded the entrance. I'd have to go through Hezekiah's tunnel to avoid detection, creating a long delay getting back to Bethany.

It was a couple of hours before I arrived. I rushed to Simon's house. The women were cleaning up as they had finished the preparations for Pesach.

"Martha, where did Yeshua and his disciples go?"

"Oh, Yeshua never goes anywhere without his trusted talmidim. They left for Pesach. Here, let me fix you something to eat," she insisted. "You look tired."

I sat and tried to relax. The house had been so full and festive the night before. The aroma from the alabaster jar lingered. I remembered Yeshua's words. I shook my head. He knew. I didn't need to warn him.

Martha placed figs and nuts on a plate and handed it to me.

We said the blessing and I ate a few bites. "Where are the disciples and Yeshua celebrating Pesach?"

They went to Bethphage, the home of Mark, to eat the meal."

"Mark?"

Martha nodded. "They wanted it to be private. There is an upper room in the family's house where Yeshua's talmidim can be alone with the Master."

"Was Judas with them?"

"Of course," Martha said. "He's one of Yeshua's talmidim."

I tried to conceal my concern.

Martha embraced my hand. "Is everything all right? You don't look well."

"I must go. Thank you for the food."

"Perhaps you can eat the Pesach meal with Mark's family, but you need to hurry."

I waved good-bye and ran towards Bethphage. How would I find his house?

By the time I arrived, it was late afternoon. The disciples and Yeshua were already in the upstairs room with the door shut. The door would remain closed until they finished the meal.

When Mark's father saw me, he got up from the table. "We are delighted to have you share Pesach with us," he said. "What a nice surprise."

He directed me to a table and Mark followed behind us. The former leper announced to the dozen or more people gathered for the festivities, "This is Daniel, son of Aviv, who used to bring food to Simon and me when we were outcasts.

Welcoming words filled the room and I felt a kinship towards Mark's family and friends. The wine flowed freely and I soon became immersed in the delicious food served by the women.

After a while, the lateness of the day pressed in on me. I'd forgotten how long the celebration takes with all the courses and recitation of prayers. I did not know how Judas would betray Yeshua, but I knew it was imminent.

When we finally finished, Mark said, "I'll be back. I want to see if Yeshua and the disciples have left."

The young boy didn't return for quite a while. Soon I heard grating sounds above us, as if furniture was being moved, and the pounding of feet on the creaking stairs. Faint voices drifted down the hallway. I kept my eyes glued to the door, filled with anxiety. The mood was festive and I didn't want to be rude. I waited patiently.

When Mark returned, he whispered in my ear. "Follow me."

I excused myself from the table and followed him outside. The air was cool and the sun had set.

"Something is amiss," Mark said.

I tried not to look concerned. "Like what?"

Mark shrugged. "I don't know. Yeshua seemed disturbed and the disciples were sad. Maybe not sad, but—tired, perhaps. They left a few minutes ago."

"Was Judas with them?"

Mark shrugged again. "I don't remember seeing him, now that you mention it."

"Did they say where they were going?"

"They didn't say, but often they go to the Garden of Gethsemane to pray at night. It's quiet and no one is around."

"Do you know where it is?"

Mark's eyes grew wide. "Will you go with me—perhaps we can find out what is going on."

"You should ask your parents."

"I will tell them," Mark said. "Wait here."

Ill at heart, I wept silently.

CHAPTER 19

S oon we were on the road. Stars covered the night sky against a full moon. The air felt unexpectedly nippy for Pesach. I asked Mark if he noticed anything unusual when Yeshua and his disciples emerged from the Upper Room.

"I've never seen Yeshua look so somber," Mark remarked.

"Did he say anything?"

Mark shook his head. "He and the disciples only sang a song as they left."

I wanted to ask which one but I let it go. "How do you know where they went?"

"They always go to the same place—the Garden of Gethsemane, to pray, on the Mount of Olives."

Have you ever gone with them?"

"No. Occasionally the women go, but not tonight. He said only the disciples."

"So how do you know where they go?"

"I've secretly followed them many times. Yeshua doesn't mind. The disciples think I'm too young."

We continued for a while in silence, following the familiar path from Bethphage. Once on the Mount of Olives, Mark took me to the olive grove on the lower western slope. The barren Judean Wilderness faced the Garden of Gethsemane to the east. Shadows wrapped the garden in darkness.

Mark started to point.

I held up my hand to stop him. "I don't want them to see us."

The olive trees in the grove provided good coverage. We could move in a little closer. I counted nine disciples. "Where are Yeshua and the others?"

Mark peered through the olive branches. "I don't see Peter, James, and John."

"I don't know the disciples that well," I confessed, "except for John, who introduced himself to me."

"James is the brother of John. Peter is the outspoken fisherman. Peter, James, and John are Yeshua's closest friends."

"Surely he wouldn't have come without them."

"Come. Let's see if they are on the other side."

We made a wide arc and circled around to the back of the garden. I tried to filter out the indistinct voices from the nighttime insect chatter.

"That must be them," Mark said.

We crept closer. A limb snapped.

I raised my hand. "Wait."

"They didn't hear it," Mark whispered. "I see three of the disciples with Yeshua."

I nodded.

What would Yeshua think if he found us here eavesdropping? This was an intimate moment between the rabbi and his disciples. Yeshua paced. The others appeared tired.

"Did you see Judas on the other side?" I asked.

Mark shook his head.

Yeshua dropped to his knees in front of his inner circle and cried out, "My soul is overwhelmed with sorrow to the point of death. I feel as if I am dying. Wait here and stay awake with me."

I clenched my eyes.

Yeshua left his inner circle and collapsed on the ground a short distance away. His words pierced my heart.

"My Father, if it is possible, don't make me drink from this cup. But let it be as you want, not as I want."

Yeshua knew. He knew. I glanced across the Kidron Valley at the Wilderness of Judea. The barren land was only steps away from the garden and a large enough area that he could hide from his pursuers. No one would ever find the rabbi in the desolate mountains. Why didn't he flee?

I studied Mark, so young and innocent. He didn't know what was about to happen. I reached out and hugged him, as much for my benefit as his.

A few minutes later, Yeshua walked back to his followers who had fallen asleep. He shook Peter on the shoulder. "Could you not stay alert with me for one hour? Stay awake and pray for strength against temptation. Your spirit wants to do what is right, but your body is weak."

James and John watched sleepily as Yeshua attempted to awaken Peter.

Yeshua returned to the same spot and prayed again.

Mark turned to me and whispered, "Something bad is about to happen."

"I know."

Yeshua knelt in front of a rock and leaned his head on it. "My Father, if I must do this and it is not possible for me to escape it, then I pray that what you want will be done."

I lamented. If only Yeshua were the son of David, the promised one.

Yeshua arose and went back to his disciples. They had fallen asleep. Again. He didn't awaken them this time, but left them and wandered in the darkness back to the same spot.

He threw himself on the ground and prayed a third time. His sorrowful cries became more urgent. They were deep, mournful, human, and frail.

When he lifted his head, red tears in the moonlight streaked his face. I wanted to approach him, to offer solace. I glanced at Mark. Tears glistened in the boy's eyes.

Mark leaned into me and whispered. "He's going to die, isn't he? I remember some of the things he said—"

I covered my mouth with my finger, signaling for him to be quiet.

Someone approached Yeshua as he lay prostrate on the ground; a large figure, perhaps eight feet tall.

"Who is that?" whispered Mark.

"I don't know."

The white translucent being embraced Yeshua. He wrapped himself around the prophet and prayed in words I didn't understand. No more than a couple of minutes passed, and then the visitor was gone.

Yeshua's demeanor outwardly changed. He now appeared resolute and determined, strengthened by the strange visitor. He immediately stood and hurried back to Peter, James, and John.

"Are you still sleeping?" he asked the men. "The time has come for the Son of Man to be handed over to the control of sinful men. We must go."

Yeshua and his three closest friends returned to the other disciples, who were also asleep. Yeshua shook them awake.

I peered across the Kidron Valley. Dozens of flickering lights formed a procession from the temple all the way to the garden. Did it require so many to arrest one man? Heartbeats filled the darkness and marching feet stomped the ground. The long-anticipated confrontation neared. The darkness of the night deepened.

Suddenly, the disciples seemed to become aware of something amiss. They quickly rose from their slumber and stared at the quivering lights. Tension saturated the air as the disciples drew near their master. I could sense the mounting terror as they peered through the grove at the hundreds of approaching men.

"Here comes the one who will hand me over," Yeshua said.

Mark unexpectedly moved closer.

I blocked him. "Are you crazy?"

"They are coming for Yeshua. We must stop them."

"No, Mark, You can't. You can't do anything."

His petrified eyes implored me, "Why not?"

"It's too late."

I peered beyond the garden to the wilderness, a stone's throw away. The rugged canyons, caves, and mountains would have provided cover for Yeshua, as it did for David when he hid from Saul, but Yeshua made no effort to flee.

The temple guards arrived behind the lantern holders and torch-bearers. In the trembling light, I could see most of the soldiers carried clubs and swords. The temple militia had trapped the disciples and Yeshua in the garden to prevent escape. I heard footsteps behind us. Other soldiers had ambushed us as well, although the olive trees hid us —for the moment.

The shuddering light shone on the faces of Yeshua and his followers, but a brief moment of indecision passed. The soldiers appeared not to know which one was the teacher.

Yeshua stepped in front of his frightened followers to shield them from the soldiers. Resolute and firm, reminding me of Commander Goren, my hero from World War II, his bravery caught the guards by surprise. They jumped backwards, intimidated by his valor.

Judas spoke up. "The one I kiss will be Yeshua. Arrest him."

Judas approached. "Hello, Teacher."

Yeshua answered, "Friend, do the thing you came to do."

Judas kissed Yeshua on the cheek.

Several of the temple soldiers seized Yeshua and arrested him. The rabbi offered no resistance. Unexpectedly Peter grabbed his sword and swung it at a servant.

Cries pierced the garden as the servant gripped the side of his head. Blood gushed between his fingers and dripped on the ground.

Yeshua shouted, "Stop!"

No one moved.

Yeshua picked up the servant's ear and reattached it. Then he turned to Peter and said, "Put your sword back in its place. People who use swords will die by the sword. I could ask my father and he would send twelve legions of angels. But everything must happen as it is written and according to the prophets."

Peter and the disciples trembled. They were unprepared for this— they never saw it coming.

LORILYN ROBERTS

Yeshua turned to face the chief priests and elders of the people who came to arrest him. In addition to the temple guards, the multitude included priests and scribes—almost everybody who was anybody connected with the temple.

I had anticipated it would be the Romans to arrest Yeshua, but the contingent was made up of his own people—the temple aristocracy.

Where would they take him?

The rabbi addressed the crowd. "Why did you come out here with swords and clubs? Am I a criminal? Every day I was with you in the temple area. Why didn't you arrest me there?"

Yeshua dropped his head. "But this is your time—the time when darkness rules."

The soldiers handled Yeshua roughly, tying his hands behind his back. Upon seeing the brutality of the highly trained soldiers, Yeshua's disciples fled. The guards let them go. They had Yeshua, the one for whom they came. Satisfied, they hauled the rabbi away into the darkness.

Suddenly, I heard rustling behind us.

"Who are you?" a voice demanded.

Mark and I turned and faced another group of soldiers that held torches and clubs. I tried to step in front of Mark to protect him, but he ran in between the guards.

One reached out to seize the boy, but only caught him by his clothes. Mark kept running, leaving his garment in the soldier's hand.

I was glad he got away, although butt naked. The guard threw the boy's robe on the ground in disgust.

Now it was only me.

"Who are you?" one of the soldiers asked.

"Daniel, Son of Aviv."

One of the guards whispered, "He's the Jewish charioteer, the one the Romans are searching for."

"Should we take him in?"

The two guards exchanged glances.

The second one replied, "What have the Romans done for us lately?"

The first one shrugged. "Leave him be. We got the one we wanted."

But the second one hesitated. "Suppose he's one of the followers?"

"He's not one of them. He was racing chariots in Caesarea."

With that, they left me behind. I watched as their torches disappeared in the darkness. Mark was gone. The disciples were gone. Yeshua—I didn't know where they were taking him, but I could see the long line of quavering lights covering the mountain. I ran through the garden to catch up.

Surely, they weren't going to do anything to the rabbi over Pesach. Maybe I was wrong—maybe it wasn't too late. Maybe history could still be rewritten.

CHAPTER 20

The reddened moon cast sinister shadows in the garden. I ran until I tripped over some roots, twisting my ankle. Hidden branches slapped me in the face and I uttered a few choice words. Why was I following Yeshua, anyway? Insanity had taken over and become a cruel, unholy truth.

Since when did priestly men arrest holy men on Pesach in the middle of the night? Didn't that only happen in Hollywood movies to evoke an emotional response?

Fiery torches lit the cool, damp air and smoke from the lanterns snaked over the mountain. The musty smell reminded me of a charred forest. The large crowd slogged through the darkness. I expected them to pass through the Kidron Valley and to enter the city. They didn't.

When I caught up to the stragglers, I recognized two of the men as Yeshua's disciples—Peter, who cut off the ear of the servant, and John. No one said a word.

A cool breeze swooped down the mountain giving me goose bumps. The night brooded in strange whispers.

I had perceived a hint of gloating by the captors when they led Yeshua off in chains. It seemed too easy. Thirty pieces of silver was hardly enough to buy a slave—the amount given by the council to

Judas. After spending three years with Yeshua, was that the paltry worth Judas attached to his Master?

Soon, we approached a large, wealthy estate, but only a few entered the gated courtyard.

"Who lives here?" I asked John in a hushed tone.

"Annas," he replied.

"Why did they bring Yeshua to him? He's not the high priest."

John shrugged. "Annas is Caiaphas's father-in-law. Sometimes I wonder who is running the temple. The priests are scouring the city for the Pharisees and Sadducees. It's highly unusual the council would meet at night—perhaps a delay tactic."

John glanced up at the moon. "It's a long time till morning."

After several minutes, the soldiers and priests reappeared with Yeshua outside the gates. We continued on what I perceived to be a death march. I knew what those were—as did every Jew in the twenty-first century.

Soon we came to another palatial home. A high wall surrounded the buildings and the courtyard.

"This is the home of Caiaphas," John said. He left Peter and me and hurried to the gate. Guards stood watch. The porter at the entrance opened the door for John. He must have known the disciple.

Most of those who had accompanied the temple guards and priests to Gethsemane were leaving. Since the prisoner was in custody, their duties were finished.

A few minutes later, John returned to the gate beside the porter, motioning for us to enter. Peter lowered his head, hunched over, as if to conceal his identity. I followed.

A gust of wind sucked the last bit of warmth from me. I tucked my hands underneath my crossed arms. A lit fire in the courtyard gave some reprieve. Peter walked over to warm himself. The embers smelled like rotten eggs.

She was here.

I looked around for the ventriloquist. Fear gripped my spirit. Only demons smelled of sulfur. I leaned against the closed gate and stared up into the darkened sky. I wasn't one of Yeshua's followers. "Why am I here, God?"

Peter turned to me and whispered, "For the same reason I am."

He was right, even if I didn't want to admit it.

I glanced around. Several apartments made up the exquisite residence. Each building faced towards the inside of the cloister. In one of the larger apartments, the temple officials had gathered. Yeshua stood bent with his hands tied behind is back. Soldiers surrounded him. I didn't see John.

The courtyard reeked of sulfur. I sneaked to the apartment where the secret proceedings had started. I felt safer inside even though I glanced back at the bonfire lighting up the courtyard. Peter still stood beside the fire warming his hands.

The demon came up beside him. Her sadistic smile conjured up horrific memories. She had been with us all along.

Peter appeared cold, lost, and confused. He needed to flee from her, but the immediacy of what was happening to Yeshua distracted me.

Caiaphas, the high priest, stood in front of the hastily called assembly. Dressed in his holy raiment, he reminded me of a hypocrite of the worst kind. He was a fraud. He was not of the lineage of the family of priests dating back to Aaron, but that didn't appear to be relevant. His title, given to him by Rome, commanded the respect of everyone who mattered.

Discordant voices filled the chambers as members of the council argued. To see men I respected resort to such ill behavior made me nauseous.

In the back of the room, Nicodemus and Joseph of Arimathea were speaking to another member of the council. John stood nearby. I edged closer to him. I asked John, "To whom are Joseph and Nicodemus speaking?"

"Gamaliel, the Elder."

I recognized his famous name from the writings of Josephus. I moved in closer to hear.

"According to the law, you can't conduct an inquiry of the prisoner in the middle of the night," whispered Gamaliel. "I quote from the Talmud. 'The members of the court may not alertly and intelligently hear the testimony against the accused during the hours of darkness.'"

"They don't seem to care about the law," Nicodemus said.

"The law also states the one cooperating in the arrest of the charge cannot be connected to the accused. Wasn't Judas one of Yeshua's disciples?"

"Yes, he was," Joseph replied.

Gamaliel shook his head.

My focus returned to Yeshua. Even if he attempted to escape, he wouldn't get far. The guards stood within arm's length of him, but he'd had plenty of opportunity to do so earlier and didn't.

Drumbeats—where were they coming from? No, they were heartbeats, like the beats on the heart monitor when General Goren died. The beats stopped as quickly as they began.

I watched as Caiaphas approached one member of the council after another. His words cut like a surgeon's knife. "Do you have any evidence against Yeshua?"

Most of them shook their head. A couple whipped up some false charges, but even the high priest knew they wouldn't stand up to the scrutiny of Pontius Pilate.

After much disagreement, two so-called witnesses came forward with a charge. "Yeshua said, 'I can destroy the temple of God and rebuild it in three days.'"

Anger welled up inside of me. That wasn't what Yeshua meant.

More discussion ensued.

Caiaphas replied, "We'll rehear the case when it's daylight in front of the council. I'm sure more witnesses will come forward about this ridiculous statement."

Gamaliel whispered, "The law states you can't immediately judge the convicted. You must go home and think about what you have heard. I suppose this is Caiaphas's way of circumventing the intent of the law for the sake of expediency."

Nicodemus asked Gamaliel, "Can you even arrest someone for a capital crime in the middle of the night?"

A member of the council who was eavesdropping accused Nicodemus. "You sound like one of his followers."

Nicodemus stared at the man but didn't respond.

Caiaphas kicked a chair. "This is not an inquiry. Yeshua will be presented before all seventy-one council members for more formal questioning at daylight."

I disagreed. The meeting sounded like an inquisition, the kind Jews had suffered throughout history.

Yeshua said nothing. Even when the high priest asked him to respond to the trumped-up charges concerning the temple, he refused to answer.

Caiaphas ordered the prisoner brought forward.

The temple guards handled Yeshua roughly. With his hands bound behind him and feet in chains, he had no way to steady himself.

Caiaphas glared at Yeshua. "I charge you under oath by the living God—tell us if you are the Messiah, the Son of God."

"Yes, it is as you say. But I say to you, in the future you will see the Son of Man sitting at the right hand of God and coming on the clouds of heaven."

Caiaphas rent his clothes in mock anguish. "He has spoken blasphemy. We don't need any more witnesses. What do you want to do?"

"He is worthy of death," almost everyone shouted.

The guards wasted no time abusing the prisoner. Their behavior disintegrated into a debasing of the kind with which Jews are familiar. The men acted like animals and spit in Yeshua's face. Another slapped him.

"Who hit you?" a temple guard jeered.

"Prophesy for us, who touched you?" a soldier mocked.

Shades of gray darkened the room, as if a light had died. I rubbed my eyes. When I opened them, I nearly fainted. Bright-red blood streaked down Yeshua's face—the only color in the room.

A cock crowed.

I peered outside at the glowing white fire and watched as Peter and Yeshua exchanged glances. Suddenly, the disciple appeared grief stricken. He covered his face and ran out of the courtyard.

I stared at Caiaphas who was no longer dressed in the priestly vestments and turban. His exquisite clothing had turned into a dark coat and extended several inches lower in the back than in the front. His grayish pants hung as potato bags around his nubby legs, and he wore a white shirt with a turned-out collar, and bowtie. He parted his hair on the right and held a hat in his left hand. His unmistakable mustache sent chills through me. The swastika on the sleeves of his jacket and row upon row of fake medals left me no doubt as to his identity.

CHAPTER 21

We entered the temple courtyard and proceeded to the spectacular Hall of Hewn Stone. Here the council's most important business took place.

Once everyone was seated, I focused on the high priest—a type of Hitler, only worse because he was one of us. The historical overlapping of the two events reminded me I was in the seventh dimension. Was time really an illusion? Even if it was, it existed. Somehow or for some reason, I was stuck in the first century. If I returned to 2015, would it be as if only seconds had passed instead of three years? I hoped.

Yeshua stood bound before Caiaphas. I had become more and more impressed with the rabbi. He knew Torah. He spoke the truth. He cared about those who had neither power nor wealth. He loved the downtrodden, the sick, and the hurting. He didn't play favorites as the Pharisees and Sadducees did.

What most impressed me, though, was his demeanor. His self-control seemed supernatural—especially now.

The judges, seven of them, sat cross-legged on comfortable cushions behind Caiaphas. The council members would vote youngest to oldest if they voted at all. That probably wouldn't happen. Why would they take a vote in a suspect proceeding?

Besides Caiaphas, among those present from the temple vanguard, the only ones I recognized were Nicodemus, Joseph of Arimathea, and Gamaliel.

The seven judges, dressed in Nazi-like clothing, could have passed easily for the Gestapo. There was Heinrich Himmler and Joseph Mengele and Rudolf Hess and Albert Speer, and even some henchmen I didn't know.

Drumbeats. Heartbeats. Time beats. I studied the faces of the temple leaders. Puffed up, arrogant, and contemptuous. This wasn't about justice. It was about an agenda. As Hitler had murdered six million Jews, the council wanted to kill Yeshua Hamashiach. More than that, they wanted him to die on a tree so they could say God cursed him.

I conjured up memories buried deep—arguments about who Yeshua was. Was he a fraud? Was he a lunatic? Was he a prophet? If he was God's son, God wouldn't allow him to be cursed by men —would he?

The grayness of the temple shadows in the early morning reflected the grayness of Pesach. Color had left the world—except for the rabbi. He was beaten and bloodied with bruises over his lacerated face. Hadn't the council shown enough disdain for the man?

At the very least, could not the judges be advocates for fairness? Would anyone speak up for Yeshua?

Sketchy witnesses waited to be summoned—pitiful examples of justice.

Gamaliel stood. "May I be heard?"

Caiaphas appeared in no mood to drag out the proceedings. "No."

Gamaliel ignored the high priest. "There has not been a vote yet."

"We don't need a vote," Caiaphas retorted.

Everyone concurred with the high priest. No vote needed to be taken.

"Blasphemy," voices murmured. "We heard it for ourselves. Case closed."

I studied the beautiful temple—it was supposed to be God's home, not a shelter for a kangaroo court. The house of God with its golden façade, white marbled columns, holy cloisters, and inner sanctum spoke of justice and righteousness. Would God render judgment on the Jewish people for the wicked actions of its leaders?

Joseph of Arimathea stood and gazed around the crowded chamber. "Suppose you are wrong?"

Caiaphas's demeanor was incendiary—inflamed, determined, and angry. How dare anyone challenge his authority. The judges shook their heads defiantly and members of the council glowered. Grumblings grew.

"He has done nothing to warrant turning him over to a pagan king," Joseph pleaded. "Have we become the hunter instead of the hunted? Have we not murdered our prophets, prophets who spoke of the one to come?"

"Are you one of his followers?" a priest asked.

He ignored the question. "Do you want his blood on your—"

"Surely you don't accuse us of such things, Joseph of Arimathea?" implored the high priest.

Nicodemus rose from his seat and stood beside his friend.

Caiaphas eyes flashed. "Yeshua's blood will be on the hands of Pontius Pilate," he spat.

For a moment, the Hall of Hewn Stone remained silent. All eyes stared at the defiant council members who stood before the high priest. That anyone would be so bold as to challenge his authority was unprecedented.

Suddenly another dimension unraveled. The fires of Auschwitz descended on the Hall of Hewn Stone. The flames engulfing the temple scorched the sacred stone as the melted gold seeped between the rocks. Chaos erupted.

Yeshua stood, unfazed. He was a man among rabid wolves—except for Joseph, Nicodemus, and the doctor of law who asked for a legal vote.

"Enough." Caiaphas straightened his bowtie and glowered as in the spirit of Hitler. "Does anyone else want to be heard?" No one in the council spoke. As far as Caiaphas was concerned, the verdict and decision stood.

Nicodemus and Joseph left. The sound of their sandals on the polished marble floor reverberated through the chamber. Another uncomfortable silence followed.

"Is Pontius Pilate ready to receive him?" a council member asked.

"He is," Caiaphas replied. "He's been warned of the urgency of the case and is waiting for us at the Antonia Fortress."

As the group left, I overheard someone whisper to Caiaphas, "Rome won't care about a charge of blasphemy."

"What charge would they accept?" Caiaphas asked.

The Pharisee whom I had seen praying in the Court of the Gentiles replied, "Did he not say, 'Render unto God the things that are God's and render unto Caesar the things that are Caesar's?'"

Caiaphas appeared to like his suggestion. "We can link it to sedition, overthrowing the government, treason, anything to ensure he's crucified and can't become a martyr."

The soldiers shoved Yeshua out of the Hall of Hewn Stone. His ugly chains dragged along the beautiful mosaic floor. I followed at a distance, hesitant to go to the place where I had once been a prisoner.

The temple choir had begun practicing as the council wrapped up the proceedings. The voices of the singers would drown out the frantic cries of the animals. The sacrificial slaughter would begin shortly.

CHAPTER 22

The temple guards led the procession with their prize prisoner bound in chains. The council and priests fell in line behind them, including Caiaphas and Annas. Nicodemus, Joseph of Arimathea, Gamaliel, John, and I brought up the rear.

As we left, Mary Magdalene joined us, along with Lilly, Johanna, and a few women who often traveled with Yeshua. The short distance from the temple to the Antonia Fortress took only a couple of minutes.

Color seeped into the temple and the courtyard, but it didn't matter. The somber mood contributed to my uneasiness. The women, huddled behind us, sobbed. John was the only disciple here. All the others had fled.

Yeshua's disciple could have offered testimony, but Caiaphas didn't allow it. Expediency prevailed.

Very few Jerusalemites were on the streets at this hour. Few knew what had transpired during the night. If the masses who had followed Yeshua had known, they would have shown up in droves to protest, but the council had planned it this way, to arrest the rabbi under the veil of darkness.

We climbed the steep steps and entered the Antonia courtyard. Here the temple guards stopped and waited. We spread out on the large platform. Roman soldiers approached and conversed with their counterparts. I was too far back to hear.

On cue, the guards thrust Yeshua towards the Roman garrison. Yeshua stumbled forwards. The soldiers backed off, probably to avoid such close proximity to one so dirtied. After a brief conversation, the Roman guards left. Again, we waited.

The courtyard appeared as I remembered it when the garrison brought me here. I never thought I would return. My mother's horror-stricken face at my arrest filled me with grief. Why would I risk imprisonment again? I didn't anticipate the Roman guards noticing me. Yeshua was their focus, but I was still ill at ease.

A few moments later, a soldier carrying a currilis appeared. He set the chair resembling a chariot without wheels in the middle of the courtyard. The guard counted off the steps.

The high priest would have told him about the required perimeter needed from the building so the Jews would be ritually clean for Pesach. I imagined Pontius Pilate irritated that he'd have to make even this small concession.

The procurator entered the courtyard wearing an impressive toga, his Roman attire for conducting official business. I had seen him many times when he dropped the handkerchief at the chariot races. He had even congratulated me once on my win. Considering his contempt for the Jews, I took it as a compliment at the time. I regretted my pride at his preferential attention in front of the jealous crowds.

Pontius Pilate sat in the currilis. He nodded at the high priest and lifted his right hand.

The proceedings began.

Even though the early morning breeze blowing towards us would make it easier to hear, I moved closer. I didn't want to miss anything. John followed me. The women lingered at the back, along with a few stragglers who had joined us when we left the temple.

Caiaphas stood in front of Pontius Pilate. His mannerisms betrayed an attempt to flatter the Roman governor. I was sure this was a devilish attempt on his part to influence the procurator's decision.

The high priest waved his hand towards Yeshua. In terse words that sounded rehearsed, he stated, "We found this fellow perverting our nation, stopping the people from paying taxes to Caesar. He even called himself the Messiah—a king!"

The crowd murmured, affirming Caiaphas's accusations.

Pilate turned to Yeshua. The man stood in chains with his hands clasped behind his back. Welts covered his swollen face. His matted, unkempt hair, dirtied by the hands of those who had abused him, hinted at the brutality of the Jewish guards. Dried blood stained his robe.

How could the Jewish high priest bring the rabbi before this heathen governor? I had lived in Caesarea. I had visited the temples of their pagan gods. I knew what sort of free lifestyle the heathen lived, filled with perverted orgies and extravagant immorality. It was bad enough the Jews had to live under Roman governance, but to bring a rabbi, one of their own, before Pontius Pilate for judgment during Pesach was unconscionable—even worse than the sham proceedings conducted in the temple.

Pontius Pilate asked Yeshua, "Are you the king of the Jews?"

The rabbi replied, "You say it."

The governor studied the prisoner.

Now I understood why God had given me the gift to read minds. I closed my eyes and pressed into the procurator's scattered, contradictory emotions.

Fear and uncertainty crippled the man. He wallowed in self-doubt over a previous reprimand from Rome involving the shields debacle. Insecurity plagued him. He didn't trust Caiaphas, and particularly Annas, who he believed to be the instigator of this whole affair.

Deep down, I sensed he wanted to be fair to Yeshua. He didn't believe the charges against the sage but felt impotent to do the right thing.

Pontius Pilate had been informed that the council would bring the teacher before him at sunrise. Though the governor had properly prepared, he was uneasy. His wife had awakened him that morning and warned him about a dream she had.

"Have nothing to do with that man," she admonished Pilate.

After his wife's warning, not only did the governor fear being recalled by Tiberius, but he also worried there was something supernatural about the holy man before him. Yet, I didn't perceive within the procurator the strength of character to release Yeshua.

I lamented. If only history could be rewritten.

I reached into my bag and clutched the magical crown and remembered what the young Jewish girl told me. Someday I would return the crown to Yeshua. Could the crown's power save the rabbi? Had I been transported back in time for this purpose?

The whole idea seemed preposterous. If only I could talk to Pontius Pilate, but he would recognize me as the former chariot racer and runaway slave. I didn't want to die.

After a couple of tense moments, Pilate faced the chief priests and crowds. "I find no ground for a charge against this man."

Caiaphas and Annas protested. "He stirs up the people, teaching throughout Judea. He began in Galilee and has brought his followers here to Jerusalem."

Pilate held up his hand for the high priest to stop. "Yeshua is a Galilean?" he interrupted.

"Yes," the high priest said impatiently.

Pilate smiled. "Then he should appear before Herod Antipas. And it conveniently happens that he is also here in Jerusalem for the Pesach."

The governor stood. "Shalom." He promptly left, leaving us standing in the courtyard. The procurator would not pronounce a verdict—at least for now.

Since when did a Roman governor address a Jewish crowd with Shalom? His tone and the way he had said it mocked the high priest. To Pilate's smug satisfaction, he had had the last word in the matter.

I touched John on the shoulder, "What is the punishment the high priest seeks from Pontius Pilate?"

John lowered his eyes. "Under our law, it would be death by stoning, but since we don't have legal standing to render a death sentence, all capital offenses must be brought in a Roman court under Roman law. In Yeshua's case, since he's not a Roman citizen, it's crucifixion. For a Jew, that means he's cursed by God."

It was as I had heard Caiaphas say. I'd hope that I had misunderstood.

With great haste, the temple guards escorted us from the Antonia courtyard. The assembly headed straight to the Hasmonean Palace. I knew very little about Herod Antipas except he had given the order for the Baptist's beheading. Time was running out for the high priest. Caiaphas and Annas fled ahead of us to the temporary quarters of the tetrarch of Galilee in the Upper City.

CHAPTER 23

We entered the Hasmonean Palace, the home of Herod Antipas when he stayed in Jerusalem on his infrequent visits. The attendants greeted us with guarded cordiality, but their uncomfortable glances at Yeshua spoke of silent apprehension. I doubted many prisoners appeared before Herod Antipas—certainly few from Pontius Pilate.

Annas and Caiaphas had warned Herod Antipas of our impending arrival. We were expected. Once the porter closed the door, the soldiers shoved Yeshua forward. His chains dragged along the marble floors and the noisy grating echoed off the walls. We crowded around and waited. Hopeful anticipation covered the faces of Caiaphas and Annas.

A few minutes later, the tetrarch made a flamboyant entrance. Exaggerated gesticulations of his hands revealed his extreme delight in meeting Yeshua.

The tetrarch plopped down in a large chair and his attendants spread out an oversized robe beneath his feet. Once the servants took their positions beside the ruler, Herod turned his full attention to Yeshua. Twirling his hand, the tetrarch smirked. "So at last we meet." He rolled his eyes. "And under such extraordinary circumstances."

Yeshua, bruised and exhausted, said nothing.

Herod took a different approach. "Come now, Teacher, I have heard much about you. In fact, I have wanted to meet you for a long time, but perhaps the reports of your miracles are greatly exaggerated."

Yeshua still said nothing. His silence put a damper on the tetrarch's enthusiasm, but Herod wasn't so easily deterred. I knew his reputation. He couldn't let this supposed miracle worker show him up.

With an air of flattery, Herod continued. "I've heard that you cast out demons."

Yeshua's appearance never changed. He stood, blood-shot eyes focused on the floor, arms behind his back, chained and bound between two guards.

When Yeshua remained silent, Herod Antipas filled the awkwardness with rambling blather, boasting about his authority, how much he liked John the Baptist—another of the rabbi's ilk—and how unfortunate it was he had to behead him.

Yeshua remained silent.

"Oh, let me see, what have I forgotten?" the tetrarch mused. He flashed his eyes at the ceiling. "Yes, you even raised a man from the dead." An awkward silence followed again when Yeshua refused to answer.

Caiaphas and Annas waited impatiently as the tetrarch rattled on at the rabbi's expense. The scene reminded me of a trapped, helpless animal taunted by bullies, only later to be slowly tortured. I glanced away, as had a paltry few others—resigned to the inevitable.

After a while, Herod must have realized Yeshua would remain steadfastly silent. The pompous ruler clapped his hands. "I insist you show me a miracle."

Yeshua never uttered a word.

I remembered being at a circus when I was young. My memory superimposed itself on the room. Another dimension had found its way here. That moment wrapped itself around this one. Time once again became an illusion.

Blue and yellow floodlights tracked through the room. Herod's servants, dressed as clowns, danced beside him. Caiaphas and Annas were string puppets. Hysterical laughter filled the room. Colorful stripes covered Herod's kingly robe and banners waved from the ceiling. A faint smell of sulfur turned my stomach. I heaved and wanted to run out of the room.

She was here.

As quickly as the strange vision began, it ended. Yeshua remained quiet, distant, and unfazed.

The tetrarch demanded once more, "Show me a miracle!" But it was to no avail. Then Herod snapped his fingers and ordered that the uncooperative guest be dressed in a royal robe.

An attendant placed an extravagant robe in the bloodied hands of Herod and the soldiers wasted no time wrapping the robe around Yeshua. The soldiers mocked the teacher, played with him as if he were a toy. I watched from the back, feeling Yeshua's humiliation, embarrassed by the soldiers' carnal behavior.

Caiaphas and Annas and many members of the council watched with smug satisfaction. The baseness of their depravity astonished me. The high priest and his father-in-law seemed like demonic puppets.

After the soldiers had had their fun and Herod had been sufficiently entertained, the tetrarch ordered Yeshua to be sent back to Pilate, better dressed than when he arrived.

Time was quickly passing and the urgency to accomplish the task wore on the faces of Annas and Caiaphas. Exhausted, I lagged behind as the assembly hurried back to Pontius Pilate.

CHAPTER 24

As we left the Hasmonean Palace, the council fanned out onto the streets of the Upper City. Their agenda was cunning, deliberate and calculated. I couldn't bear to listen to their wiles.

I watched as Pharisees rushed to the temple. Others scoured the roads and alleys. The temple vanguard needed a "paid" audience at the Antonia Fortress. Thousands of men participated in the affairs of the temple. Caiaphas was desperate to curse the rabbi—even if it took all of them to convince Pilate.

I hurried to catch up with John, Gamaliel, Joseph, and Nicodemus. Several more women had joined our group. As I thought about the women who had met Yeshua, I could not think of one who ever rejected him. Shale would have been here with us.

I climbed the steep staircase to the fortress. At least a thousand had gathered, waiting for Pilate to begin.

A soldier brought the currilis out to the stone pavement, as he had done before.

The governor strode out into the courtyard. Impetuous disdain covered his face. I read Pilate's mind. How dare the high priest interrupt his day again with this supposed rabble-rouser.

"Have nothing to do with that man," his wife had said.

Caiaphas approached him.

Pilate glanced around. "Where is the rest of the council?"

Caiaphas shrugged. "It is the Pesach. Many have gone to prepare."

Liar. The priests were recruiting Jerusalem lowlifes to influence the procurator's decision.

"Surely this trial is more important," the governor snapped.

A slight delay ensued while the Roman and temple guards rounded up the council.

When the delayed proceedings started at last, the number of people had doubled. I stared into the eyes of those recruited. A biased crowd, purchased by the temple treasury, to persuade a pagan king to kill a man. But Yeshua wasn't any man. He was a prophet sent by God. The question stood, at least in my mind—was he more than that?

I smelled sulfur. She was here. The familiar feeling of unsettledness swooned over me, making me nauseous.

Once all the members of the council were present, Pilate sat in the chair of judgment.

He waved his hand at Yeshua and addressed Caiaphas. "You brought this man before me on a charge of subverting the people. I examined him in your presence and did not find the man guilty of the crime. Neither did Herod because he sent your prisoner back to me.

"Clearly, he has not done anything that merits the death penalty. Therefore, what I will do is have him flogged and released."

As if on cue, the people shouted, "Crucify him, crucify him."

All of the women shouted back, "No, release Yeshua."

I joined my voice with theirs. Yeshua had never stirred up the people against Rome or told them not to pay taxes to Rome.

I noted Caiaphas had subtly changed the charge from blasphemy to treason, as I had overheard him discussing with the unidentified priest when we left the temple.

John, Nicodemus, and Joseph of Arimathea joined me, shouting for the release of Yeshua.

Pilate stood indecisive, tentative. Did he possess enough fortitude to see through the lies? Was he willing to risk a riot or bad report to Tiberius if he set an innocent man free?

Despite the protests of our small group, the voices of so many drowned us out.

"Put him to death on the stake," the crowd roared.

The procurator raised his hands. "It is a custom each year for Rome to release a prisoner during Pesach as a token of our good will. Who should I release, Yeshua Barabbas or Yeshua who is called the Messiah?"

"Give us Barabbas," the crowd shouted.

Pilate would not have been able to anticipate this outcome. He did not know this was a paid temple crowd.

Pilate ordered his soldiers to flog Yeshua. As I watched a weak-willed man succumb to compromise, I found myself thrust into another place, far into the future, though instantaneous and fleeting.

A president stood on another stone pavement. Surrounded by dignitaries who were Asian, European, Jewish, and Arab, I felt the treachery of broken promises and compromise. Pontius Pilate was one of many world leaders given the power to do great things for God's people. He wouldn't be the last to fail.

As the guards hauled Yeshua away, I ran towards the front. I knew what I must do. I knew where they would take him. With all eyes on Yeshua and so many gathered around the stone pavement, no one noticed me as I slipped inside. Unwanted thoughts intruded on mine. The soldiers each wanted to scourge the prisoner.

It was now or never. I thrust the crown towards Yeshua.

The guards, shocked at my sudden appearance, stood frozen—or perhaps time stopped. I didn't say anything.

Love without measure, poured out, pierced my soul.

Hands lunged at me from all sides. As soon as I felt them, they let go. Something stronger yanked them away.

I heard a voice. "Run."

I bolted through a passageway as the guards moved in slow motion. Finding a cave hidden in the rock wall, I squeezed into the small enclosure. I remembered the hidden passageway near the dungeon too late.

Running boots down several nearby corridors signaled they were hunting for me.

"That was Daniel, the Charioteer," one guard said.

"Forget him," another one replied, "Let him go. Pilate wants us to take care of this one."

A few minutes later, the flogging began. Yeshua's cries filled the fortress. I buried my face in my hands and wept. "Why, God?"

I had hoped the secret powers of the crown might save him. It was a futile attempt at the impossible.

His loving eyes lingered in my memory—if only he could be the Messiah. My Jewish friends from 2015 told me it was impossible, but they hadn't seen what I had seen.

The jeers of the soldiers having too much fun filled the fortress. Their laughter at Yeshua's expense was maddening.

Why didn't he save himself?

More wails followed.

I shook uncontrollably.

After several agonizing minutes, the beating stopped.

"Put this purple robe on him," one of them said.

"Here's a crown," another one smirked.

Could it be mine? No. I had seen them stomp on it as I ran away.

Shouts filled the fortress. "Hail, king of the Jews!"

I heard more laughter.

More cries.

More moans.

Tears rolled down my face.

Why, God? Why? If God heard me, he was silent.

Yeshua's chains dragged on the stone pavement.

Gasps erupted from the crowd.

Again, Pilate asked, "Who should I release, Barabbas or Yeshua?"

The crowds shouted, "Barabbas."

Pilate replied, "You take Yeshua and put him to death. I don't find any case against this man."

A voice shouted, "We have a law. According to that law, he ought to be put to death, because he made himself out to be the son of God."

Silence followed.

Once again, chains dragged on the stone pavement. Pilate must have brought Yeshua back inside the fortress, away from the roaring crowds.

Pilate asked, "Are you king of the Jews?"

Yeshua replied, "Is this your own question, or did others tell you about me?"

"Am I a Jew?" Pilate asked. "Your own people and leading priests have brought you here. Why? What have you done?"

Yeshua answered, "I am not an earthly king. If I were, my followers would have fought when I was arrested by the Jewish leaders. But my kingdom is not of this world."

Pilate replied, "You are a king then?"

"You say I am a king, and you are right. I was born for that purpose. And I came to bring truth to the world. All who love the truth recognize what I say is true."

Pilate asked, "What is truth?"

Yeshua didn't respond.

Footsteps paced back and forth.

Minutes passed.

Pilate asked, "Where are you from?"

Yeshua remained silent.

Pilate raised his voice. "You refuse to speak to me? Do you not realize I have the power to set you free or to have you crucified?"

Yeshua replied, "You would have no power over me if it hadn't been given to you from above. This is where the one who handed me over to you is guilty of a greater offense."

Shouts from the mob outside intensified.

"If you set this man free, it means you're not a friend of the emperor. Everyone who claims to be a king is an enemy of the emperor," someone shouted.

I closed my eyes. Pilate could not ignore such a claim.

The chains dragged. Yeshua was taken outside again.

"Here's your king," Pontius Pilate announced.

The crowd shouted, "Take him away. Take him away. Put him to death on the stake!"

Pilate asked, "You want me to crucify your king?"

Caiaphas shouted, "We have no king but the emperor."

I flinched. It was for that reason Caiaphas had handed Yeshua over to Pontius Pilate.

I heard nothing. Minutes passed.

"Bring me a bowl of water," Pilate demanded. As he dipped his hands in the water, he addressed the crowd, "My hands are clean of this man's blood; it's your responsibility."

The crowd cried out, "His blood shall be on us and on our children."

The procurator issued a command. "Have a sign written and posted on the stake, Yeshua from Nazareth, the king of the Jews. Write it in Hebrew, Latin, and Greek."

Was it all over? Wouldn't they allow for more witnesses? Many did not yet know about the proceedings.

The fortress became quiet. I waited a long time. Rather than risk capture sneaking out the front, I wanted to run down the staircase to the dungeon.

I peeked around the pillar. Could they have taken Yeshua down there? I didn't know what to do.

Indistinguishable voices filtered through the front entrance. Some had lingered. I fled down the steps. No one saw me, much to my relief. When I arrived at the cell, only a couple of men remained imprisoned. I didn't want to talk, but one prisoner reached out and snatched my robe.

"You were right," he gasped.

I shook my head. "I don't know what you are talking about."

"Barabbas was released a short while ago, as you said."

I stared into the empty cell.

"Let go of me," I demanded.

His grip tightened.

"Who are you?" the man asked.

"It's not important."

The prisoner let go. "You are a prophet."

I backed away before he tried to clutch me again and tore through the narrow tunnel. I thanked God for the secret passage back but I no longer had the crown. How could I get through it without any light?

"Please help me, God," I whispered.

As I entered the tunnel, snakes hissed and slithered under my sandals. I bolted through the darkness, stepping on some of them. Unexplained laughter echoed through the passageway. This time it was more than the voice of the ventriloquist I heard. I sensed she had brought along her friends to feast on the merriment.

I hated my sarcasm, but who was the real enemy in all of this? Was it the Romans, the council, or demonic spirits? Satan's lair was inhabited by more than just snakes.

"Please protect me, God," I cried.

Within a few minutes, I reached the temple mount. When I opened the door, sunlight poured inside the opening. Thousands of pilgrims milled about. The temple visitors had no idea what had happened during the night or at the Antonia Fortress.

I charged into the Court of the Women and peered into the men's courtyard. To my surprise, Judas was there, along with some of the priests.

Sacrifices would begin shortly. The Levite choir had gathered.

I glanced around.

Where had they taken Yeshua? Wouldn't the high priest hold him at the temple until after Pesach?

A disturbance erupted outside the temple walls. Discordant voices cried out and running feet pounded the street. I started to go see, but the dinging of coins reverberated inside the cloister. A huge plume of smoke reached into the heavens above the temple.

Judas fled past me. His eyes bulged as a man possessed. In his haste, he almost knocked me over. Thirty pieces of silver covered the temple floor in front of the altar.

CHAPTER 25

Bright red blood flowed from the temple down into the Brook of Kidron. The temple smelled from the savage slaughtering. We had forgotten the enormous cost. The deaths of innocent animals made us right with God—but only temporarily. The sacrifices had to be repeated—again and again.

I fled past the temple cloisters and courtyards and exited through the Eastern Gate. Judas had disappeared in the crowds.

The choir sang.

I glanced up the road. Condemned men carrying crosses approached. I knew them. My knees knocked. I wanted to turn away, pretend I hadn't seen them.

Perhaps I would have if it were not for the man who followed them. A laser pierced my heart, peeling back layers of regret. If only things could have been different.

Yeshua lagged behind Gestas and Dysmas. The guards slapped the rabbi with a whip. Jeers went up and the temple vanguard pressed forward for a better view—adult entertainment for depraved minds. Annas and Caiaphas smirked as Yeshua struggled to carry the cross.

The teacher, weakened from the scourging and abuse, tripped. Disgust and disdain covered the faces of his enemies. Yeshua dropped further behind. The Roman soldiers became impatient. As the rabbi approached the Eastern Gate, the guards seized an unsuspecting visitor.

"Hey, you, carry the cross of this condemned rabble-rouser."

A few minutes passed while the guards affixed the piece of wood to the traveler's back. He protested.

"What is your name?" the soldier asked.

"Simon from Cyrene. I have traveled a long ways to celebrate Pesach."

"You'll have plenty of time to celebrate after this man is nailed to the stake."

The procession exited through the Eastern Gate and continued beyond the walls. Straight ahead, three stakes stood at the bottom of a hill.

Pilgrims crowded along the sides of the road.

Yeshua's friends cried.

His enemies gloated.

John stood beside Yeshua's mother and Mary Magdalene. Nicodemus and Joseph were nearby. Next to them was the paraplegic I had promised I would help. I failed him. Yet the man stood on both feet —Yeshua must have healed him.

When the rabbi saw the women beating their breasts, he said, "Daughters of Jerusalem, don't cry for me. Cry for yourselves and your children. For the time is coming when people will say, 'The childless women are the lucky ones—those whose wombs have never borne a child, whose breasts have never nursed a baby.'

"Then they will begin to say to the mountains, 'Fall on us!' And to the hills, 'Cover us.' For if they do these things when the wood is green, then what is going to happen when it's dry?"

Was Yeshua referring again to the destruction of Jerusalem?

As a visitor from another time I knew that forty years later, flames would pour out of the temple. The Romans would kill so many Jews, they would run out of wood.

The words shouted by the crowds in front of Pontius Pilate haunted me. "His blood shall be on us and on our children!"

SEVENTH DIMENSION - THE CASTLE, BOOK 3

Did the council bring judgment on future generations by their shameful, wicked actions?

The Roman guard slapped Yeshua. "Move on."

Mary Magdalene dropped her face into her hands. The other women reached out to support her.

The council, having accomplished their black-hearted deed, could get on with Pesach.

The prayers of the choir reached us beyond the city walls. The perpetual sacrifice would take place shortly.

Look upon our affliction and plead our cause…for you are a mighty redeemer….

The music took the edge off the cries of dying animals, but nothing would silence the words of Yeshua. Not even death. Two thousand years into the future, millions of Christians would hear his voice and follow him while the Jews still waited for the Mashiach. If only Yeshua had been the chosen one. If only.

The execution site was on a busy roadway into Jerusalem. The Romans had dug a cemetery a few meters away—as an insult to the Jews.

"What is the name of this place?" I asked John.

"The Skull, Golgotha."

The soldiers worked quickly. A Roman centurion stood guard as the garrison did their jobs. One after the other, they stripped the men and nailed them to their crosses. The condemned souls cried out.

God would never allow such suffering to happen to his son or the son of David—would he?

I leaned over and asked John, "From what tribe does Yeshua belong?

John whispered in my ear, "The tribe of Judah."

Must be a coincidence.

It was the third hour—nine in the morning.

The soldiers staked Yeshua between two criminals—my former prison inmates. The only sounds now came from the weeping women and the condemned men as they struggled for air.

Yeshua cried, "Father, forgive them. They don't know what they are doing."

Tears flowed from my eyes. How could he be asking God to forgive these men?

The soldiers divided up Yeshua's clothes. A one-piece robe was a novelty. The men threw dice to determine who would take it.

I remembered another time—when guards stripped Jews and stole possessions. Fires filled the sky. The condemned walked a similar Via Dolorosa. Death was too soon for too many. Murdered at the hands of men who hated, taking what they wanted. Watches, gold, rings— wicked hooligans who stole what wasn't theirs.

I glared at the Pharisees, Sadducees, and priests. Why did Yeshua allow them to do it? He could have saved himself, but he chose not to.

As people passed, they gaped at the condemned men. The rubber-neckers fancied a peek. How many secretly gloated at the expense of the condemned men?

The sign on Yeshua's cross read, "This is the king of the Jews," written in Hebrew, Latin and Greek.

Murmurings in the crowd became more vocal. Some of the Phar-isees and Sadducees jeered, "Behold the man. He saved others. If he is the Messiah, the one chosen by God, let him save himself."

Another scoffer rebuked him, "Aha! So you can destroy the temple, can you, and rebuild it in three days? Save yourself."

The soldiers laughed, shrugged, and went back to playing dice. One stuck a sponge of vinegar on a stick to his mouth. Yeshua refused it.

Another of the Torah teachers made fun of him. "So he is the Messiah, the king of Israel? Let him come down from the stake. If we see that, then we'll believe him."

Voices cried out, "If you are the king of the Jews, save yourself."

Gestas, who hung beside him on the left, hurled insults at Yeshua. "Aren't you the Messiah? Save yourself and us."

But Dysmas spoke up and rebuked Gestas. "Have you no fear of

God? You're getting the same punishment as he is. Ours is only fair. We're getting what we deserve for what we did, but this man has done nothing wrong."

He turned to Yeshua. "Lord, remember me when you come into your kingdom."

Yeshua replied, "I say to you, today you will be with me in paradise."

The rabbi gazed towards us. Yeshua spoke with great difficulty. "Woman, behold your son."

John was standing next to Mary.

He said to John, "Behold your mother."

My eyes filled with tears I couldn't hold back. He took care of his mother better than I took care of mine. Yeshua's kindness convicted me. I had left my mother during an attack—sneaking out of the apartment without telling her where I was going. What was my mother doing now?

I glanced at Mary, Yeshua's mother. What sorrow God had chosen her to bear. How could she ever forgive those who had sent her son to the cross?

It was now noon, the sixth hour.

I was tired of all the taunting. He had saved me in the fortress. He had healed Nathan. I had seen him bring a young girl back to life. Others had witnessed him raise Lazarus from the dead. Why didn't he save himself?

A gradual darkness descended. No solar eclipse would be possible on Pesach—not during a full moon.

Nicodemus whispered, "From the Scriptures, it is written in Amos, 'I will make the sun set at noon, I will darken the earth on a sunny day. I will turn your festivals into mourning.'"

I made a mental note to check the scroll of Amos. Then I remembered the scroll of Daniel I had found in the temple. I wished I had asked the rabbi if he could unseal it when I had the chance.

Hours passed in silence. Many shook their heads and left. Most of the priests stayed, probably to ensure there was no foul play. All the women remained, as well as Joseph, John, and Nicodemus.

It was the ninth hour, three in the afternoon.

Yeshua cried out, "Elohi! Elohi! L'mah sh'vaktani? My God, My God, why have you deserted me?"

Some said, "Look, he's calling for Eliyahu."

I gathered a stick and one of the sponges nearby, soaked it in vinegar, and gave it to him to drink. His eyes met mine, fleetingly.

Several rebuked me.

"Wait," one demanded. "Let's see if Eliyahu will come and take him down."

Yeshua let out a mournful cry and uttered his last words from the cross. "It is finished. Father, into your hands I commit my spirit."

The Roman officer supervising the crucifixion exclaimed, "This man truly was the son of God!"

From the temple, the choir sang as the perpetual evening sacrifice took place.

"You, O Lord, are mighty forever, you revive the dead, you have the power to save…"

A low-pitched rumble shot up from underneath the ground. Suddenly the earth moved beneath my feet.

"Earthquake!" a man shouted.

Crowds swarmed around me as they tried to escape the perceived danger, fleeing into the countryside away from the affected area. Seconds later, the cemetery next to the condemned men split open.

Terrifying sounds poured out of the temple as boulders fell. Thunderclaps bolted through the darkened sky. I fell to the ground as frightened observers fled. The blackness spread.

As I lay on the ground, I watched the temple shake. Then I saw him. He stood on the precipice. His deep reddish coat shone despite the darkness—as spectacular as the lion I saw when I first arrived—the lion from the tribe of Judah, the root of David, and the fourth son of Jacob. I glanced at Yeshua—if he was the son of David, could he be—

A Roman soldier shouted, "Hey, you, Daniel, the Charioteer!"

I jumped. Too late, I realized my mistake. The Roman soldier aimed the spear at me, but I scrambled to my feet and bolted. The dusty air from the quake settled in my throat, making me panic. What if I couldn't breathe? Only when I reached the entrance to the city did I glance back. The soldier had stayed with the garrison. It was only a matter of time.

The sooner I left Jerusalem, the better. There was nothing keeping me here. Pesach would be over soon. If the Roman soldiers caught me, they would crucify me—the death sentence for runaway slaves. Having just seen how they relished that task, I had no desire to join them.

In the outer temple courtyard, boulders had fallen on the stone pavement and pillars had crumbled. Columns lay in ruins. Dust and debris covered everything.

Temple priests brushed past me into the Court of the Gentiles blabbering, "The temple veil is torn, top to bottom."

More chaos followed.

I tiptoed closer. The earthquake had obliterated the Chamber of Hewn Stone—the meeting place of the council. I knew the chamber would never be rebuilt. An epiphany revealed a deeper truth—the last order the council issued from the temple was to crucify Yeshua.

I stepped over fallen boulders and balusters littering the mount. I could barely get my breath. I hurried through the Court of the Women, up the stairs, through the damaged Nicanor gate, and into the Court of Israel.

Terror stricken, more priests fled. Hundreds had been in the cloister sacrificing animals when the quake struck.

The desolation in the temple area reminded me of the deserted streets in Israel following attacks on our people—a grisly reminder of the tenuousness of our existence.

Squalls of wind that sounded eerily like temple shofars blew dust in my face. A few crows circled overhead. I peered into the Court of the Priests covered in sacrificial blood. Beyond it, the torn veil revealed the Holy of Holies.

I drew nearer and closed my eyes, hoping to feel God's presence. "Help me to understand," I mouthed silently.

A lion roared. I opened my eyes and saw the magnificent creature in the Holy of Holies. Slowly, he morphed into a lamb. Blood trickled down his sides.

Terrified, I ran back outside the courtyard. I stared at Golgotha. I watched as the soldier broke the legs of Dysmas and Gestas to speed up their deaths.

When the soldier came to Yeshua, he didn't break his legs. He stabbed the spear into his side. Water and blood gushed forth.

I remembered Dr. Luke, my old mentor. I would go see him. He would help me to understand everything.

After a few minutes, the soldiers took Yeshua down from the cross and handed him over to Joseph of Arimathea. Nicodemus stood beside him.

Was Joseph a relative? I never thought to ask. The women, huddled together, followed them.

I was too afraid to help Nicodemus and Joseph prepare Yeshua's body. The guards would arrest me. Nicodemus was carrying a heavy bag—probably myrrh and aloes for the rabbi's burial.

I walked slowly back into the temple courtyard. Despondency made me weak, taking away my last remaining hope of returning to 2015.

I had made no sacrifice to God and I had not changed history. Instead, I had failed, if that was what God had sent me here to do. I was a complete and utter failure. I had seen an innocent man put to death—a rabbi who the world was not worthy of.

When I gazed straight ahead, through the dust and debris, I saw the dog. I ran to him, thankful not to be alone.

CHAPTER 26

I started to pet the animal on his head, but he jumped up and buried his paws in my chest. The dog's whimpers stirred my heart—he needed a friend as much as I did—and I reached around and embraced him. Wet kisses covered my cheek—so typical of a dog—and a pleasant surprise after so much sadness.

I glanced up at the temple. No one was near me.

I chuckled and rubbed his furry head. "Who are you? If Shale were here, she could talk to you."

The dog wiggled out of my arms and ran to the stairs. He stopped at the stairwell and barked.

"You want me to follow you?"

The dog wagged his tail.

I followed him as he disappeared down the steps.

Fog covered the stairwell and the steps disappeared into a thick white soup. I ran my fingers along the edge of the scroll in the bag as I descended. A shofar blew.

When I reached the lower mount, the smell of horses filled the platform. The fog cleared, and a dark blue neon light radiated from the pillars, shining brightly upon the area.

Across the mount, horses stood in dozens of groups under high arches framed by tall columns. The area, known as Solomon's stables, wasn't used for horses until the Crusades. How could they be here? I walked past rows of animals, including camels—hundreds of them.

I was in an overlapping time warp.

The dog barked again and ran farther into the darkness. I followed him. After several minutes, I stumbled upon a beautiful white horse. I approached the animal and stroked his neck.

Resting my head on his shoulder, I asked, "Are you the one?"

He nudged me with his nose.

The dog barked again. I searched for a saddle and found one hanging on a column.

After mounting the horse, I followed the dog through more arches and double columns that continued for several acres. Darkness made it difficult to see how big the platform was, but thousands of animals filled the underground temple mount. The shofar blew again as I approached the gate to exit outside.

Sunlight blinded me momentarily, and when I glanced back, the time warp had closed. I had returned to the first century.

The dog ran away from me and I followed him on the horse. Why did he head towards Golgotha? I didn't want to go that way, but I followed him anyway.

Outside the Eastern Gate and beyond the city walls, the empty stakes stood as silent witnesses. The spectators to the holocaust were gone. The dust had settled and the place was eerily quiet. Only bloody splotches from the crucified men covered the ground, a grisly reminder of the first holocaust.

Next to Golgotha, the dog sprinted around the cemetery. People sat beside open, empty graves. Seven ghost-like wraiths smiled and waved. They glowed in a white translucence with hands held towards the sky. The dog greeted the apparitions and became as radiant as they were, sashaying around each of the phantoms.

I watched for several minutes—stunned. Then the shofar blew one more time and I peered up at the darkened sky. A strong breeze stirred as clouds whipped across the heavens. I gazed at the cemetery, mesmerized, until the dog and the phantoms faded away. It was as if the wind had pulled them into another dimension.

A flock of birds flew overhead, breaking my trance.

If Shale had been here, she could have talked to the dog and told me everything. My longing to see Shale had deepened. How would I explain to her what had happened to Yeshua? So often, she had shared with me about the king and I had refused to listen.

I must return to Galilee. I could stop by Dothan on the way and visit Dr. Luke.

I procured the reins and thumped the horse's hindquarters with my heels. "Let's get out of here," I muttered, and we took off towards Dothan.

CHAPTER 27

The setting sun and the appearance of two stars marked the beginning of Pesach. I didn't know how far I could travel on this day according to the Torah, but I no longer cared.

Over two years had passed since I had been to Dothan. The roads were empty. As I approached Jacob's Inn, hunger pangs became an obsession. It didn't help remembering all the good meals I had enjoyed at the inn. I had no money. How did I plan to pay for my room and meals? I didn't want to ask Dr. Luke for a job again.

I tethered the horse next to the stable and approached the portico. No one was outside. I had arrived here from 2015 on this very porch. I walked over to the chairs where my friends Ami, Levi, and I used to sit and talk—where they found me, confused, and with a contusion on my forehead. I reached up and touched the healed scar. I still didn't remember how I received it.

The inn would not be expecting visitors today. Most families had gone to Jerusalem for the festival. Those who couldn't travel would stay with families—except for Dr. Luke's patients. The old, infirm, and sickly would always have a home here, courtesy of Dr. Luke and the inn's owner. A kind man he must be.

I sat in my old chair, reminiscing. Soon I dozed off.

Ami and Levi's voices awoke me—a pleasant reminder from the past.

Ami greeted me first. "You have come back to visit us, Daniel of Aviv."

"No, Daniel, the famous charioteer," Levi corrected.

Ami waved his hand and leaned back. "It's all the same to me."

I smiled. "It's great to see both of you."

Levi tapped his cane on the stone pavement. "Doctor Luke will be delighted you have returned. You were missed."

"So he is still here?"

"Busier than ever," Levi said, "except for the leper colony. Yeshua healed all the lepers."

Levi's young brother, Ami, leaned towards me. Questions popped from his alert eyes. "Did you come from Jerusalem?"

I nodded.

He lamented. "I haven't been to the temple for Pesach in years. Maybe someday."

"First I must talk to Doctor Luke." I glanced at the entrance. "Have you any unleavened bread for Pesach?"

Levi waved his cane. "Get something to eat. Tell Jacob to bill me. He is in town for Pesach, and you should see if they have any rooms available."

"Are you sure?"

"For you," Levi said.

"Thank you."

I went inside. The lobby hadn't changed. Wooden chairs and tables filled up the dining area. Flowers in stone jars decorated the tabletops. The sun shone brightly through the windows and a gentle breeze kept the room cool. There was something reassuring about sameness.

I walked up to the check-in counter to inquire about a room.

The attendant was cordial. "I will check and see if we can extend you credit," she replied.

I hated to ask her to bill Levi for my room. "For a night or two."

"We have one room available for VIP's," she said. "Through the door, third room on the right."

"Thank you."

"Here's the key."

"Oh, one last thing."

"What's that?" the attendant asked.

I have a horse tethered out front."

"Yes, sir. We will see to your horse. When the owner returns from Pesach, you can work out the billing."

"Thank you." I hated to impose on Levi.

I sat in the dining area. A young woman set a plate in front of me. "Levi told me to bring you some unleavened bread," she said, smiling.

"Thank you." The woman must be new here. I didn't remember her.

Soon I felt someone's presence behind me. When I turned around, a big grin covered Dr. Luke's face.

"My old friend," the doctor said.

I stood to greet him. The doctor had a few more wrinkles and a little less hair, but other than that, he hadn't changed.

"It's good to see you, Doctor Luke."

"And you too, Daniel. Your fame precedes you."

"I'm not racing chariots anymore."

"The Romans have been here. They said you were a runaway slave."

"It's a long story," I confessed.

"Can you stay a while?"

"I have much to talk about with you."

Dr. Luke waved his hand. "Never mind the Romans. Theophilus is my friend and he gave you a good report."

I had forgotten Cynisca and I had spent the night with Theophilus before I came to Jerusalem. "I sent Cynisca to Galilee with the horses. I feared for her safety, but there is other more pressing news I must share with you."

Dr. Luke assured me. "I want to hear. I will come to your room after the meal is finished."

"I'm in the third room to the right."

"The same room you had before," Dr. Luke reminded me.

He was right. The same room I had before.

CHAPTER 28

I lay down for a quick nap, but I could neither sleep nor stay awake. A big pot of coffee would have been nice, even though I'd forgotten the taste of java. Recollections from Pesach permeated every thought, and I was tired—tired of being in the first century. Three years is a long time to be stuck in the wrong time or wrong dimension or anywhere besides home.

I sat up and rubbed my eyes. Why didn't Yeshua save himself? Nothing could have stopped him—nothing, if he had wanted to live. Was I missing something—something important?

If Yeshua came back to life, as Christians claimed, I would reconsider everything my Jewish friends had told me.

I opened my bag and took out the scroll. The letters in Daniel's name were faint and hard to read. Would I ever be able to unseal the book?

My mind was too preoccupied to sleep. Why was it that my mind wanted to sleep when I yearned to think? My one consolation—the demon would never find me here.

It was early evening before Dr. Luke and I had a quiet moment together. The women had cleared the dishes and some of the men lingered, indulging in desserts and discussing business.

Dr. Luke joined me at our habitual table by the window. The lanterns along the walls quivered—eerily similar to the flickering shadows in the Garden of Gethsemane.

We had not spoken in over two years. When I arrived from 2015, I didn't have a beard and my hair was shorter. I had also grown a couple of inches taller and gained muscle mass from chariot racing.

Dr. Luke's first question surprised me. "How is the cut on your forehead?"

I pulled my hair back. "Can you see it?"

He rubbed his finger along the scar. "Not bad for such a nasty wound—in the shape of a cross."

I didn't want to think about crosses.

Dr. Luke smiled. "No one will notice it except your future wife."

I laughed. I still didn't remember how I received the mark. After an appropriate pause, I changed the subject. "Are you aware of what happened in Jerusalem during Pesach?"

Dr. Luke cocked his head and raised an eyebrow. "Should I be?"

"Yeshua died at the stake."

Dr. Luke's eyes appeared grief stricken. "What?"

I shared with the doctor the details, how the council had turned him over to Pontius Pilate and how the procurator had tried to free him, but in the end, Pilate had succumbed to the demands of the high priest.

Dr. Luke stood and paced the dining hall. A couple of men stopped him on the arm. "Are you all right, Doctor Luke?"

He nodded. With shoulders slumped, he leaned over the table and whispered, "Please excuse me. I'll be back in a few minutes."

"All right," I replied.

Levi, clutching his cane, ambled over to my table. His voice was so loud everyone could hear him. "What's the doctor upset about?"

Everyone peered at me.

"Yeshua died at the stake yesterday in Jerusalem, outside the city gates."

Listeners gasped.

Ami broke the silence. Lifting his hand, he declared, "Behold, the Lamb of God, who takes away the sins of the world."

I didn't expect Ami to preach. "What do you mean?"

He dropped his hand. "John the Baptist said about Yeshua, 'He is far greater than I. I'm not worthy to lose the strings on his sandals.'"

I remembered the vision of the lion turning into a lamb. "Does that mean John thought he was the Messiah?"

Ami choked on his words. "The priests killed the Baptist. Now they have killed the Messiah."

"How can he be the Messiah if he's dead?" Levi asked.

Another man said, "Good riddance. He couldn't have been the Messiah."

A voice responded tersely, "Why do you say that?"

"He was a threat—he led the people astray. He ridiculed the religious leaders. He stirred up trouble everywhere he went."

"He didn't stir up trouble," another interrupted. "He healed the sick."

"The only people who claimed he was the Messiah were the uneducated, the downtrodden, and those who wanted something from him."

"That's not true," someone else argued.

The banter continued and I regretted the conversation. What good could come out of this except to stir up strife? I'd seen and heard enough conflict in Jerusalem—I didn't want to listen to it here.

One of the cooks entered the dining hall from the kitchen. "It's very simple," the woman said. "We'll know if he's the Messiah if he comes back from the dead."

A couple of men snickered at such a preposterous idea.

Silence followed.

A few minutes later, the dining room cleared. Some probably disagreed with the woman's statement, but out of respect, they remained silent.

I sat alone for a long time. Would Dr. Luke return? I had given up and was leaving to go to my room when he appeared.

"Sit," Dr. Luke said. "Sorry for my delay."

I chose the same chair at the table by the window.

Dr. Luke cleared his throat. "Tell me everything you know. Don't leave out anything."

The doctor had brought paper and a pen for note taking. Into the early morning hours, I told Dr. Luke everything I knew. He asked few questions. He just listened and wrote.

When I finished, I glanced at his copious writing. "What are you going to do now?"

Dr. Luke replied, "The most excellent Theophilus and I have had many conversations about Yeshua."

I remembered what Theophilus told Cynisca and me before we left Caesarea.

"I will put this information in a scroll. I'd like to talk to Mary, some of the women who knew him well, and his close friends. I regret I never had a chance to meet the Master."

The doctor leaned back in his chair contemplating the terrible news. "But he healed many—the entire leper colony. We must preserve the record of his accomplishments."

I wanted to ask Dr. Luke his opinion before the opportunity passed. "Do you believe Yeshua was the Messiah?"

"Was or is?" Dr. Luke shook his head. "I can't believe he's gone. What message did Yeshua send to John the Baptist?"

I ran my hand through my hair. "I don't know."

Dr. Luke tapped his fingers. "Herod imprisoned John the Baptist for a couple of years. Shortly before Herod beheaded him, John sent Yeshua a question. He asked, 'Are you the one or should we look for another?'"

"What did Yeshua tell him?"

"He sent word to John through friends. 'The blind receive sight and the lame walk.'" Dr. Luke's lower lip trembled. "'Lepers are cleansed.'"

I put my hand on his arm. "I know two of those lepers."

The doctor continued. "The deaf hear, the dead are raised up, and the poor have good news preached to them."

I sat back in my chair. "I've seen his miracles, Doctor Luke, and much more, but I also saw him die on the stake. Wasn't the Messiah supposed to restore Israel? Yeshua could have, but he didn't. Why not?"

Dr. Luke shook his head. "I don't know."

We sat in silence.

I held up my bag. "I have something to show you."

Dr. Luke perked up. "What's that?"

I handed him the sealed scroll.

Dr. Luke examined the outside of it. "Where did you find this?"

"At the temple."

"Wait a minute." Dr. Luke disappeared and returned a minute later with another scroll in his hand. He laid it on the table. "Open it."

I began reading. "It's the scroll of Daniel, isn't it?"

"Yes. Read what it says at the bottom."

I skimmed over the last several lines. "I heard and did not understand, so I said, 'My Lord, what will be the outcome of these things?' He said, 'Go, Daniel, for these words are secret and sealed to the time of the end.'"

I glanced up from my reading. "Do you think this is the book he references?"

Dr. Luke stood and put his hand on my shoulder. "Perhaps, but we should get some sleep. I only wanted you to think about it."

"I will, Doctor Luke."

"We'll talk more, all right?"

"Thank you." I handed him his scroll and put mine back in the bag.

Dr. Luke paused before leaving. "The cook is right. We will know —soon enough."

CHAPTER 29

Loud banging on the door awoke me. I stumbled out of bed and slid over to open it.

"Are you still asleep?" Levi asked.

I stuck my head outside. Blinding sunshine seeped into the hallway from the lobby. I squinted. "What time is it?"

"Past mealtime. Are you all right?"

I rubbed my eyes. "Dr. Luke and I stayed up late talking. I need an alarm clock."

"A what?"

When were clocks invented? "Sorry, bad joke."

Panic rose in my gut. "The Romans?"

Levi tapped his cane. "You think I'd wake you up to tell you that?" The old man shrugged. "If she comes by again, do you want me to show her to your room?"

My knees quivered. "A she?"

Levi's eyes danced. "Probably an admirer of yours."

"Can you describe her?"

Levi leaned on his cane. "Long, brown hair, fair skin, gorgeous."

It couldn't be Cynisca. Her hair wasn't that long. Lilly didn't know

I was here. Martha—she didn't know I was here either. Shale—that was ridiculous.

"I have no idea who it could be. Is she coming back?"

Levi shrugged. "Get something to eat. When she returns, you can greet her yourself."

"I'll be out in a few minutes."

I watched as Levi meandered down the hallway with his cane. Should I bring my bag? I decided to hide it in the secret compartment underneath the table. The map was still there from three years ago so my bag should be safe.

I sat at the table by the window in the dining hall. It was the second Shabbat of the week, still considered Pesach until sundown. The unknown visitor must be a gentile. Several hours passed and the woman didn't return.

The setting sun and the appearance of the first stars marked the end of Pesach. With the festival over, the rawness of events in Jerusalem faded, but not as much as I had hoped.

I strolled out to the portico. A cool night breeze blew and darkness covered the streets. Whoever came to see me earlier must not be coming back. My heart sank not knowing who the mystery lady was. Some friend from long ago must have changed her mind. I started to go inside when I heard a female voice.

"Daniel!"

I searched the darkness. Shale stepped out of the shadows—as beautiful as ever. She ran up to me and I embraced her ravenously.

Her smooth, gentle skin tingled. Her body melted in my arms, swallowed up by my embrace. Her heart raced next to mine—sending me into a roller coaster of elation and joy and stupor.

I stepped back to study Shale's perfect features. "What are you doing here? I mean, how did you know I was here?"

Shale's eyes twinkled in the flickering light from the portico. "I had a hunch."

I had so many questions I didn't know which to ask first. I glanced behind her.

"Did you bring any belongings? Where is Baruch?"

Shale dug her head into my chest. "Later. I want to rest in your arms."

I laughed. Could I be dreaming? If so, I never wanted to wake up.

I sneaked a peek at her hand. Did people in the first century wear wedding bands? "Did you and Judd get married?"

Shale sighed. "Must you ask so many questions? Just hold me. The long journey tired me."

I clasped her tighter. I glanced up at the dark and empty road. Did she walk from Galilee?

I reluctantly let go of her and motioned her to follow me to the portico.

"We can talk over here."

We sat at my favorite table. The gentle breeze and the low light of the torch reminded me of sweet times. Shale's long brown hair rippled against her shoulders. Perhaps it had grown a little longer. Grace and beauty had lavished their resources on Shale.

Shale wistfully flipped her hand. "Why did you leave Caesarea?"

"To go to Jerusalem. You found me and I can't imagine how. You knew I was in Caesarea?"

She smiled. "I have my secret sources."

I couldn't stop staring into her piercing green eyes and admiring her clear fair skin. She was smitten with natural beauty, more alluring than even a movie star.

Shale leaned forward and whispered, "Let's run away together, you and me. No one will ever know."

I chuckled uneasily. Did I feel that way, because I so powerfully wanted to go with her, or because I still worried about what people would say?

Shale tossed her hair gracefully over her shoulders and sat back. "Right now. Tonight."

Her unpredictability hadn't changed.

I tapped my fingers nervously. Was she serious? "Shale, let's slow down a little. I haven't seen you in over a year."

She glanced towards the inn. "Do you have a room here?"

"Yes. I was on my way to Galilee—to see you and Cynisca, and—to take care of business."

"Can we go to your room—and be alone?"

That seemed a little forward even for Shale.

I cautioned her. "We must protect your respectability."

She waved her hand in the air. "Who's going to know?" She scooted her chair closer to mine and placed her hand on my thigh. "Daniel, you have no idea how much I've missed you."

I placed my hand on top of hers and glanced back at the inn. "I missed you too."

Shale whispered, "I want you to hold me forever."

As much as I wanted Shale, we needed to talk. "Something happened in Jerusalem over Pesach."

She pulled her hand away. "What?"

"Yeshua was hung on a stake. He's—gone."

Shale seemed nonplussed. She lowered her head and her eyes studied the portico stone slab. "Is that all you have to say to me? Haven't you missed me?"

Had she changed that much?

"Take me to your room," Shale urged. "Where we can talk in private."

Someone opened the front door to the inn. I sat up straight.

I didn't know the man, but I smiled when he greeted us.

We didn't speak until the inn guest disappeared down the road.

Shale scooted her chair even closer. She was still needy but in a different way. I liked her better the way she was before.

I tried to engage her in conversation. "Shale, we need to talk—about important things."

She sat back and pouted. "What do you want to talk about?"

"You didn't marry Judd? I mean, I don't see a ring on your finger."

"A woman can be married and not wear a ring, you know."

"So are you running away from Judd? Did he hurt you?"

Shale started crying. "You don't love me anymore."

I leaned over and touched her gently on the arm. "Of course I love you. You know that."

"Can't you hold me for a minute? I haven't seen you in a long time and I traveled for hours to be with you."

Was I being insensitive? I'd thought she would be more interested in Yeshua.

Shale tucked her body in closer. "Why don't you get your bag and we can run away together."

I grimaced. "I lost my money."

Her hand caressed mine. "Oh, I don't care about the money."

I felt uncomfortable but I didn't know why.

She whispered longingly, "I love you."

Something wasn't right. Unexpectedly, I smelled sulfur on her breath. I scooted my chair backwards, flipping it over.

Shale clutched the chair with both hands, surprised by my abruptness.

Her shocked face grieved me. My head spun and I struggled to speak. "You aren't Shale Snyder."

The shape shifter seized. My unexpected insight had stunned her, like a frozen computer program, but she wasn't a robot—she was living. Robots didn't smell. Soon her body morphed into a dark and inky glob without form. I could hardly bear to look at her now. The deception was cruel. While I couldn't read her mind—which meant she couldn't be human—I could feel her nakedness. She needed a body. No doubt she used a lot of energy to deceive me and present herself in the appearance of Shale. Why was she so desperate? A few seconds later, she materialized into the ventriloquist.

My heart pounded inside my chest. "You—you monster!"

She laughed with her familiar toothy smile and waved her bony finger. "I almost had you. Next time."

Flames leaped out of her bulging red eyes. I bolted from the portico and fled inside. My whole body burned, as if on fire. What had she done to me? I clutched a bucket of water from the dining area and flung it over me. The inn guests ogled me, bewildered.

I poured water over my arms and legs. I was half-drenched, but at least the burning stopped. Maybe it was all in my mind. Coldness now seeped into my skin. I stumbled to the window and searched for the demon.

Shale called out to me. "Help me, Daniel, please."

The urgency in the voice of the real Shale startled me. I couldn't read the ventriloquist's mind.

Levi wobbled into the dining room with his cane. He flinched when he saw me. "Are you all right?"

I ran over and clasped him, almost knocking him to the floor. "Where is Doctor Luke?"

"Did you check his room?"

I let go. "Sorry." I raced down the hallway and tried to compose myself as I banged on the doctor's door.

Dr. Luke opened it.

My clothes clung to me like a wet rag. "I'm sorry for bothering you. Shale is in trouble. I must go."

Dr. Luke agreed, "By all means."

"Can you promise me something."

Dr. Luke lifted his eyebrow, "What's that?"

"Check out Yeshua's claims. I told you everything I know—except one thing."

"What's that?"

"I must know if he comes back to life." I couldn't believe I had uttered the words, but after witnessing the shape shifter turn into a demon—what if Yeshua's death happened to reveal something greater —something that would shake me to the core? I needed to know the truth.

"You will write an accounting of everything?"

Dr. Luke smiled. "I told Theophilus I would. And with your help, I know more now than before."

The doctor paused. "I want to know the truth about these things as you do."

"Thank you. It—it's very important."

"Why are your clothes wet?"

"I—I was hot."

"Are you sick?"

I shook my head. "No."

The doctor handed me a dry tunic. "I will pray for you and Shale. Let God's hand be upon both of you."

"Thank you."

"Give Shale my kind regards."

I hugged the good doctor and ran to my room. After I changed, I snatched my bag, turned in the key, and left riding on the white horse. I started to gallop towards Galilee but something stopped me. I listened. Shale was calling to me from Jerusalem. How could that be? I desperately needed Dr. Luke's prayers. I checked repeatedly to make sure no one was following me.

Moss-laced trees looked like bearded spirits from the underworld. Limbs took on the shape of deformed hands groping in the darkness for unsuspecting victims. A black hole had suctioned up all the stars and the full moon cast the only light. Moving shadows stalked as demons who smelled of sulfur.

The ventriloquist was here.

The pounding of the horse's hoofs as we galloped to Jerusalem reassured me. I was still alive even if everything else appeared dead.

Memories from Pesach tormented me—the cruelty of the council, the mocking of the soldiers, the disdain of the Romans, the lofty arrogance of the leaders. It didn't matter if they were Romans or Jews. They were like Nazis—a well-oiled machine designed by imaginative, satanic ego-driven monsters. I hated this century.

Why, God, why are you keeping me here?

Shale's voice became louder and clearer. Nagging insecurity and memories from the halfway house tormented me. An accusing voice ranted, "You are crazy."

I clasped the reigns and urged the horse to go faster. We tore through Ramallah and arrived at the outskirts of Jerusalem in the middle of the night. I slowed down when I sensed Shale's presence nearby, but I didn't see her.

Was I insane to search for a girl I hadn't seen in over a year in a remote area of Jerusalem before dawn?

Something on the ground caught my attention. I dropped from the horse and followed animal prints, a person's footprints, and other unidentifiable prints along a trail from the road. After I tied up the horse, I followed the prints to a hidden cave. Vines and overgrowth blocked the entrance. I stopped to listen.

CHAPTER 30

Shale's voice escaped through the cave opening. "No, Cherios, you mustn't die."

I ran my fingers through my hair. Thank goodness she was still alive.

Sobs followed.

I cleared away the branches and bolted inside. Columns of freezing air that emanated from green neon rocks along the walls pelted me. A couple of dragon-like creatures flew by. I lunged deeper inside—and the curse of cold air lifted.

I stopped to listen.

"What? What do you mean—the garden and the apple tree?"

Other indistinguishable sounds followed.

Shale spoke again. "She's a garden bunny. She wants to go home."

Suddenly I slipped and fell. A few choice words escaped me, but I kept following Shale's voice. When I reached the end of the tunnel, she stood holding a white rabbit with her dog and donkey beside her.

Her eyes widened. "Daniel! What are you doing here?"

Was it really her? Goosebumps covered my skin. "I read your mind. I told you before, the next time I wouldn't delay if I thought you were in trouble."

The dog flashed her bushy white tail and ran excitedly up to me. I patted Much-Afraid on the head and rushed over to Shale. "Are you all right?"

Shale dropped her eyes. "I think so, but Cherios isn't. We must get her back to the garden, but I don't know the way."

Baruch, the donkey heehawed.

Shale wiped tears from her eyes. "We need to go to the olive garden in Jerusalem. That's where Cherios asked to be buried."

I stared. "You mean the Garden of Gethsemane?"

Shale nodded.

I shook my head vehemently. "You don't want to go there. Violence erupted in the garden the other night. The temple guards captured Yeshua. The council held a meeting and accused him of blasphemy. Pontius Pilate crucified him at the stake."

Shale closed her swollen eyes. "So it is true."

I wrapped my arm around her shoulder. "The place is crawling with guards. There are stories about Yeshua returning from the dead. You don't want to go there. Bury Cherios someplace else."

Shale asked again, as if not convinced. "He is dead?"

"Yes. I'm sorry. They placed a sign on his stake, king of the Jews."

Shale cried unashamedly.

I soothed her as best I could. "I'm sorry," I said again.

Shale cradled the lifeless rabbit in her arms. The furry creature appeared small and insignificant now that she was gone.

Much-Afraid whimpered some more and I patted her on the head.

"Let's get out of here." I directed the animals and Shale back to the cave entrance.

Once outside, Shale reached out to stop me. "Daniel, I heard what you said, but we have to take Cherios to the olive garden."

I sighed. "If that is what you must do. We better hurry and do it before daylight."

"I'm sorry," Shale said.

I reassured her. "Let's go." I lifted Shale onto Baruch's back and mounted my horse.

Before leaving the cave, I wanted to know. "Shale, what's the name of this horse?"

She asked the animal and the horse neighed.

"Truth."

"The horse's name is Truth? Who would name a horse Truth?"

Shale bit her lip. "Who gave you the horse?"

"I think God did."

"Is God not truth?" Shale asked.

Enough said. Much-Afraid trotted behind us. We didn't speak again for a while, but I sensed it wasn't an ordinary night.

Shale remarked, "The underlings are everywhere."

"I know." The overwhelming smell of sulfur gagged me. I imagined demons escaping out of hell and plundering the countryside.

Shortly before arriving at the garden, Shale said, "Daniel, there weren't any apple trees in the garden. A wolf almost attacked me here. I'm afraid."

I didn't remember seeing an apple tree either. "Why would Cherios tell you to take her to the apple tree in the garden if there wasn't an apple tree?"

Shale fidgeted. "I don't know."

A private conversation followed between the donkey and Shale.

"What is he saying?" I asked.

"Baruch said Cherios ate his apple. It's been, what, three years? Maybe the apple tree grew from the seed."

The full moon had begun its descent when we reached the edge of the garden. Posted along the border was a guard.

I whispered to Shale, "I'll distract him so you can sneak past. Give me about fifteen minutes and I'll meet up with you."

Shale nodded.

CHAPTER 31

After tethering Truth to an olive tree between the garden and the wilderness, I hurried back to the front entrance.

How could I distract this Roman soldier? I listened to his thoughts. He was anxious for his watch to end. I needed to do something so Shale could slip past him unnoticed.

I crouched behind some olive trees and tried to send him a thought. "Wouldn't it be nice to take a walk through the Kidron Valley."

I waited. Apparently, my mind-reading ability didn't translate into telepathy—but it was worth a try.

I couldn't delay any longer. I called out to the guard in Latin. "I saw the Jewish charioteer head towards the Kidron Valley a short while ago."

The guard jumped and scanned the darkness. "Show yourself."

"No time. Hurry or you won't catch him."

The soldier hesitated.

"I sprained my ankle. Take the trail to the city."

The guard lifted his eyes towards the Kidron Valley.

I spoke with authority. "Don't let him get away. I'll stand your guard."

The soldier saluted me and scurried down the path.

I cringed. The salute reminded me too much of the Nazis. A minute later, Shale entered the garden riding on the donkey. My heart pounded —suppose the guard returned too soon?

I heard a branch snap. I glanced behind me and peered into the orange eyes of a savage beast. I eased back from the creature. A hissing snarl left his curled lips. I grabbed a stick and waved it at him. "Get out of here!"

The wolf backed up, but his wild eyes smelled blood. What advantage could I have against a killer who could see in the darkness better than I?

I watched the torch sway in the wind at the guard's station. Could I reach it? The animal approached me again. I threw my hands in the air and thrust the stick at him. He growled louder.

I slogged in the darkness towards the torch. Every few seconds, I thrust the stick at the wolf.

Footsteps.

The guard's station was too far away.

I picked up a rock.

I waited as long as I dared. I flung the stick towards the man, shouted at the animal, and hit the wolf with the rock. The wild beast yelped and scampered away—and I hightailed it in the opposite direction. A few seconds later, the soldier's cries pierced the garden. I flinched.

I ran until I felt something slam into me. Then the ground dropped. The force of the collision sent me tumbling down a steep hill.

When I awoke, the sun had risen in the sky. How much time had passed? I glanced up the hill and saw a dead body hanging from a tree. The man's intestines had split open and his insides were everywhere. Then I saw his face.

I threw up. I had collided into Judas—he hung himself. Now I was defiled. I stood and checked my arms and legs. Nothing was broken, but I had a splitting headache. Since I had touched a dead body, I couldn't go back to Shale—I would defile her, too.

More worrisome to me was the probability that once the authorities found Judas's body the soldiers would scour the area. I needed to get Shale out as soon as possible.

I retrieved Truth and galloped to Bethany. When I arrived at Simon's house, no one was outside—not even children.

I knocked on the door.

Martha peeked out—until she recognized me and then flung the door wide open. "Daniel, what are you doing here? Come in. It's not safe on the roads."

Inside, I saw many of Yeshua's followers—men and women who had supported his ministry. What would they do now that their leader was gone?

Mary slammed the door and locked it.

I echoed their sentiments. "I'm sorry."

I sat apart from a young woman so as not to defile her, but she reached over and reassured me. "He is risen."

I brushed back my hair. "What?"

"It is true—even if no one believes me."

"I believe you, Mary of Magdala," Martha said.

"I do, too," Martha's sister, Mary, said.

"The disciples didn't," the woman lamented.

Lilly tried to encourage her. "Give them time."

Lazarus spoke up. "He said on the third day, he would rise from the dead. Why should we be surprised? He raised me from the dead."

More discussion ensued.

Feeling terrible about my defilement, I walked over and asked Lilly, "Can you get me a clean tunic? This one is dirty. I need to return to Jerusalem as soon as possible."

Lilly grinned. "You smell awful."

"Oh." I hoped no one else noticed.

She whispered, "Come with me to the kitchen."

A few minutes later, she provided me what I needed. "Thank you," I told her several times. I couldn't thank her enough.

When I walked to the door to leave, Lazarus touched my arm. "Be careful."

I nodded.

Simon added, "Mark fed and watered your horse."

"Thank you, Brothers, for everything."

Once outside, I hurried over to Truth. Mark greeted me warmly. "Your horse is watered and fed."

I squeezed him on the shoulder.

He eyed me sheepishly.

I grinned. "I'm glad you're safe."

He smiled. "Me, too."

Simon stood in the doorway and waved good-bye. All I could think about was Shale.

CHAPTER 32

When I reached the crest of the Mount of Olives, despite the damage from the quake, the gold columns from the temple still glistened in the morning sunlight. Could Mary of Magdala be right about Yeshua?

I tied Truth to the same tree as before on the edge of the garden and imagined the brouhaha that would erupt when the Romans found two dead bodies—the guard and Judas. I detoured all the way around to avoid the guard's station and entered from the other side.

Much-Afraid ran up to me wagging her tail. I patted her on the head. I followed Much-Afraid and found Shale standing in a quiet corner. I was grateful she was still here.

Even though Shale appeared to be alone, I knew that she wasn't. Her dark brown hair reached halfway down her back and her colorful dress shone in the filtered sunlight.

I had almost reached her before she noticed me.

I threw up my hands and apologized. "I'm sorry I didn't return last night. I was detained."

Shale draped her arms over my shoulders but didn't say anything. Was something about to happen? Too many things I wanted to tell her. Her words confirmed my worst fears.

"I must go, Daniel. It is time."

Was there nothing I could say to delay her?

"I guess I came to say good-bye." I heard my voice crack and wondered if she noticed.

She leaned in to me. "I wish I'd asked the angel about you. I was saving you for last, but I ran out of time."

I stroked Shale's shoulders trying to think of what to ask first. My mind was filled with too many questions and so little time. I glanced around but could not see an angel—apparently a gift God had given her but had not given me.

Shale interrupted my thoughts. "My father, how is he?"

How long had it been since I'd seen Shale's father? She didn't know I had been racing chariots. She also didn't know her father was married to someone else. I doubted Mr. Snyder would return to Galilee any time soon. For Shale's sake, I lied. "He's fine."

"Oh, Daniel, I hate to leave. But the angel said we would meet again."

"An angel?" If only I could see him.

Shale squeezed me tighter. "Daniel, you must believe the king is the Messiah. Your life depends on it. He's risen."

I laughed nervously. "Risen?" I didn't want to confess to Shale she might have been right all along. I was a Jew from 2015 and Jews didn't believe Yeshua was the Messiah. He did not set the Jews free. He did not become their king. He did not fulfill the Messianic expectations, but I didn't want to discuss that with her now.

I reassured her. "I'll be helping Doctor Luke. He wants to do an investigation into the king's claims. I know there is something different about the rabbi. I want to learn the truth."

Shale smiled. "Will you be at my father's house or in Dothan?"

"Both." I gently lifted Shale's head. "A mystery is hidden in all these events, but I know I will understand later."

I remembered my cousin. "Tell Rachel shalom when you return to Atlanta."

Shale smiled. "I will. My best friend hears all my secrets."

I reassured her. "I want to learn more about this man of God."

"I'll find you in Israel," Shale promised.

I grinned. "I have no doubt you will."

Shale reminded me, "I'm seventeen now. I've been here three years."

And I reminded her, "I'm from your future."

Shale swallowed hard. "You need to be back by 2015 to meet me. You will be back?"

"Do I control that?"

Shale replied, "Yes. Believe."

"Believe?" If only Shale knew what that meant.

Shale stated emphatically. "Daniel, he is risen. The evidence is all around you. See Cherios—where is she, anyway?"

I glanced around to look for the animal.

Shale laughed.

The rabbit was sitting on Baruch's back.

"She's alive—how can she be alive?" I asked.

Shale's words revealed much wisdom.

"It is easier to believe in things we see than to have faith in the power that is unseen, but the things we see are an outward manifestation of that power. Believe me when I tell you."

I hugged Shale tighter. "I will."

I needed to know. "So you and Judd never married?"

Shale shook her head. "I could never marry him."

I breathed a sigh of relief. I felt better hearing it directly from her. There was still hope, then, for us. But would I even make a good husband? I certainly had not been as good a friend to Shale as I should have been.

She stepped back. "You will take care of Baruch and Lowly?"

"Lowly?"

"The pig."

Only for Shale would I do such a thing. Right now, I would do just about anything for her. "Of course."

Shale's sadness seemed too heavy. "Aren't you excited you are going home?"

Her lips trembled. "Without you."

My heart ached. I brushed Shale's hair back from her face. "You are more beautiful each time I see you."

Shale laughed. "I almost forgot." She reached into her dress pocket and pulled out two golden nuggets. "These rocks have burned almost everyone else, but I don't think they'll hurt you." She handed me one.

I flipped over the stone. The gold luster reminded me of the temple facade. "Is it gold?"

Shale shrugged. "Keep the nugget. My promise I'll find you in the future. The angel assured me I would."

"The angel? You keep talking about an angel."

Shale turned. "He's over there. You don't see him?"

I shook my head. "I wish I did—if only. I believe you, though."

"You must believe, Daniel. Your unbelief is holding you back."

I wanted to believe Yeshua was the Messiah. But the cost—separation from my family, expulsion from the synagogue, rejection by the Jewish community, ostracism from my friends.

"Oh, Daniel. I just remembered something important."

"What?"

"Promise me you will go into my private room at my father's and retrieve my writings. I left them and I don't want my stepmother to find them."

"Your writings?"

"My diary, my scrolls. Keep them until we meet again."

I chuckled. Could Shale have written something about me? "Can I read them?"

"If you can't resist, but don't let anyone else. Promise me you will keep my writings safe?"

"I promise."

Shale picked up Cherios who had hopped over to us.

"Daniel, how will you get back?"

I didn't know—yet. "As you will, through the door."

"The portal will close soon, the angel says. The time has come."

Shale gave Cherios one last hug and put her down. The little rabbit hopped over and kissed Baruch and Much-Afraid and gave Shale and me a wink.

A few meters away, a round doorway opened, as if a small hole had been created that led to another dimension. I wasn't too far from the truth—I saw a beautiful garden on the other side.

Cherios excitedly hopped through the portal. A plethora of rabbits greeted Cherios as soon as she was discovered. In an instant, a dog ran up and joined the crowd of animals.

"Fifi is alive!" Shale exclaimed.

I didn't know who Fifi was.

"Cherios never told me she knew Fifi," Shale said.

Silence followed, as if Shale was talking to someone I couldn't hear.

Shale said, "I couldn't forgive myself, so I never told anyone my secret."

What secret did she mean?

I stole closer to her and wrapped my arm around her waist. More animals surrounded Cherios. We were missing a spectacular party in the king's garden. Soon the image faded away.

Much-Afraid, groomed to perfection, stood beside Shale.

Shale exclaimed, "Wow! You are stunning. Did Baruch lick you clean?"

Much-Afraid pranced in front of us, showing off her shimmering white coat.

Baruch heehawed.

Shale smiled. "Baruch, you're so sweet. You'll always be my favorite donkey."

"Are you ready, Much-Afraid?" Shale asked.

I didn't know Much-Afraid was going with Shale.

Shale and Much-Afraid stepped towards the door and Shale waved hesitatingly. "You promise to wait for me, right? And get my diary?"

"Yes. I will see you in 2015."

CHAPTER 33

A gust of wind sheared the ground and spiraled up into a swirling cloud. Shale's long brown hair danced across her shoulders. A soft light fell across her face and a sweet smile graced her lips. With outstretched arms and palms facing upwards, she lifted her eyes towards the heavens.

"No," I cried. "I want to go with you."

I ran up and touched her arm. As my fingers reached her, she faded into nothingness. A strong gust of wind knocked me off balance. I rubbed my eyes, refusing to open them, knowing I would be all alone.

Exhaustion seeped into my body and other aches and sore muscles complained, but all that mattered was Shale. When would I see her again?

When I opened my eyes, I didn't recognize my surroundings. The bluish-green room contained living things, but I didn't know what they were—either gigantic humans or supernatural beings. Some of them had many eyes. I couldn't see the faces clearly except for the one in front of me.

A voice said, "Daniel G. Sperling."

The large supernatural being, seven feet or more, wore a shiny black robe and appeared important and powerful. He pressed in on me, violating my space. He vacillated between poring over an ancient book and peering intently into my eyes.

"I still don't see your name," he said at last.

Another even more impressive creature came forward, dressed in a bluish-white shimmering robe. "You are too soon."

The black-robed creature glared. "He's had three years in this wasteland of indecision."

"That's right," the other creature replied. "He hasn't made a decision."

The supernatural being with the old book gritted his teeth. "He's mine."

"You can't have him—yet. He has a little more time."

The first creature stomped his foot and waved the book. "This is the book. His book is irrelevant."

"Your power is diminishing, Lucifer."

Lucifer snarled. "I'm still the prince of the air, Michael."

So they were angels.

Michael raised his hand. "Daniel's soul has been purchased."

"His death is imminent," countered Lucifer.

I stared at the two arguing. My heart burned and I sweated profusely.

"I'm not ready to die," I cried out.

The two stopped.

Michael came closer. "When you stepped into the portal you stepped out of the seventh dimension and into the place of judgment.

"I—I was following Shale."

"You still have more time in the seventh dimension—to make a decision. Shale's future is sealed. Each person must make the journey, but you can't follow her path any more than she can follow yours."

"I want to go back to my time in 2015. I don't know how to return."

The archangel studied me. "If you return now, your odds of accepting God's gift will diminish. Each time you turn away or reject the truth, your heart hardens."

I didn't have a hard heart. "What do you mean?"

"God gives each man and woman the choice. Perfect love allows free will, but each decision precludes other choices that might have been wiser. God knows the outcome. The process is for your benefit, to reveal what's in your heart.

"Your value is immense in the future and Lucifer knows that. You still have a little time. If you forfeit this opportunity, God will choose another one to take your place."

"Put like that, I want to return to the seventh dimension. I—I want to be in God's will."

"You have been shown much, Daniel."

I nodded.

Lucifer thrust the book in front of me. "Your name is not written in the book of life. You are mine despite what Michael says."

I couldn't bear to make eye contact with the fallen angel. What did I need to do to get my name in the book? Could someone tell me?

Michael interrupted the serpent and spoke reassuringly. "Lucifer doesn't have the finished book. Nor is he omnipotent or omniscient. As the father of liars, his knowledge is limited."

I glanced from one to the other.

The good angel spoke. "Finish your journey. You won't remember this when you return. God's mighty warriors are praying—the real battle for people's souls is supernatural. You are highly esteemed, Daniel. Keep seeking the truth."

"How do I get back?"

"Close your eyes and pray."

When I opened my eyes, nothing appeared familiar, but I sensed I was no longer in the garden. In front of me was a cave.

When I stood, I ached all over.

Somebody approached. I ran and hid.

A Roman official accompanied by two men in chains became visible. Another guard brought up the rear. The four men stopped at the entrance to the cave.

One of the prisoners said, "We rolled this huge boulder up to the entrance. It must weigh four thousand pounds. And we sealed it to make sure no one moved it—even if they were strong enough."

The official picked up a rock and slammed it on the ground. "Yet it was moved. How did the rabble rouser escape? A dead man doesn't climb out of a grave."

"A thief stole the body," one of the men said.

"Did you fall asleep?" the official asked.

"No, we did not fall asleep. We took turns sleeping. Someone was always awake."

The official glared at them. "How could someone have stolen the body if you didn't fall asleep?"

They exchanged glances. "We don't know."

"We must make up a story," the official said. "We'll tell Pilate Yeshua's disciples stole his body. We'll give you money to keep quiet, and you can pray you aren't executed for leaving your post."

One of the soldiers insisted, "He was gone when we left. We didn't leave our post."

"You ran away," the official insisted, "like cowards."

Silence followed.

One of the men remarked, "See how the boulder is rolled away. Up a slope, not back from the entrance but away from the entire sepulcher. It would have taken several men to move it that distance. How could no one have heard anything? Other guards were nearby."

The official smirked. "So the rock moved on its own. Yeshua's disciples slipped in and stole his body, even though you were awake and saw no one?"

"We didn't fall asleep. There must be another explanation."

The official fumed. "You can give that other explanation to Pilate before your execution."

The officials stomped off with their imprisoned former guards. After a couple of minutes, their voices faded in the distance.

The urgency to get Shale's diary made me impatient to leave, but my body didn't want to cooperate. I ached all over, including my head, but I was also anxious to examine the empty tomb. How fortunate I was to have stumbled upon it.

Before I moved, another person approached. I stayed hidden.

Soon I saw Mark riding on Truth.

I waved at him from behind the trees. "What are you doing here?"

He trotted over to me. "I found you at last."

"What are you doing here?" I asked again.

"Well," Mark stammered. "I wanted to follow you. I lost you when you galloped away, but I had a feeling you were going to the garden. I didn't find you there, but I found your horse."

Mark was too smart for his own good.

"After hearing what Mary of Magdala said, I wanted to visit the tomb. Alas, I find you here."

"You seem to have a habit of secretly following people," I remarked.

The boy dismounted. "Only people I care about. Besides, someone was about to steal your horse. I ran him off."

I sighed. "Thank you. I didn't think about that."

I had an idea. "Mark, would you like to keep Truth for a while?"

"Truth?"

"The horse."

"Sure," Mark replied.

"I need to go to Galilee and return Baruch to his owner."

"Who is Baruch?" Mark asked.

"The donkey. He's near the garden entrance. And you can't follow me to Galilee."

Mark laughed. "I have no desire to follow you to Galilee. That's a long way."

I nodded.

Mark glanced at the tomb. "Did you check inside the sepulcher?"

I shook my head. "No. The Romans just left a minute ago. I haven't had a chance."

"Let's go see." Mark ran over and I followed.

All that remained was Yeshua's grave clothes. The wrappings were in the position of a body, slightly caved in, and empty.

"It's like he left his clothes behind," Mark commented.

"You would know about that, wouldn't you?" I responded.

Mark turned red in the face. "That's not funny, you know."

I ran my hand through my hair. "You're right, Mark. I'm sorry."

Mark shrugged.

I shook my head. That was poor comic relief. "I feel nervous being here. It's too weird."

"I know," Mark said. "It's creepy."

I put my hand on his shoulder. "We need to leave before they discover something else."

"Like what?"

"Don't ask." We lingered for a moment longer. Mark wasn't ready.

"Mary must be right," exclaimed Mark. "I had to see for myself."

"Which way is it to the garden? I'm worried about Baruch."

"How can you not remember?" Mark asked.

"I hit my head yesterday when I fell. It affected my memory." That was partially true.

"Follow me," the boy replied.

We returned to the garden and found Baruch waiting in the back where Shale and I had left him.

"Do you want some apples?" Mark offered. "I found these."

"Sure."

He pulled out several and handed me one. He also gave some to Truth and Baruch. "Donkeys love apples, too."

As I put the apple in my bag, distant voices filled the garden. How long would it be before they found Judas's body and the dead guard?

"Mark, we need to leave. Promise me you will take Truth and go back to Bethany now?"

The boy nodded.

I helped him on the horse. "Thank you for taking care of Truth."

"I'm glad to," Mark replied.

I slapped the horse's rear and watched as they cantered away. Once they disappeared, I mounted Baruch.

"Let's go, hurry."

The donkey barely moved. I'd forgotten how slow donkeys were.

But at last, he did move—at a donkey's pace. When we reached the main road to Galilee, his slow speed didn't matter. Hundreds of weary travelers were also traveling home.

While I was grateful for the crowds to help hide me from the Romans, getting there quickly was another matter. We would need to stay overnight in Dothan as the trip to Galilee would take longer than I anticipated.

CHAPTER 34

Travelers filled the crowded road and rumors swirled about Yeshua's death in Jerusalem. After three days of laborious travel, I stopped in Dothan at Jacob's Inn to rest.

We had finished dinner and some of the men stayed to discuss the latest news. Gossip traveled fast in the ancient world even without the internet and television. Ami was the first to ask about my trip.

He began the night's discussion. "Daniel, is it true Yeshua is alive after being hung on the stake?"

Why did Ami ask such difficult questions? I set my drink on the table and leaned back. "I talked to a woman, Mary of Magdala, who claims to have seen him."

The room erupted with doubt and skepticism. "That can't be true," one man said. "Nobody can come back from the dead."

"But Yeshua raised a man from the dead, didn't he?" a voice countered.

"No, it was a young girl he raised from the dead," another replied.

A man slammed his fist on the table. "Caesar! What intelligent person could believe such nonsense? Are you foolish men here?"

Levi raised his hand. "Daniel, do you have any evidence besides what the woman said? We can't always trust women."

Every eye focused on me, as if ready to attack me if I said something stupid.

"Well, I did visit his tomb the day following the second Shabbat. The seal was broken, and someone had moved the stone."

Everyone remained silent.

I glanced around the room. "The tomb was empty. The Roman guards insisted no one had removed the body."

Another voice chimed in. "Why did the Romans allow the tomb to be opened?"

The air was getting hot with controversy. Several talked at once and I fanned my face.

Ami raised his voice over the others, "Daniel, what do you believe happened?"

I studied the faces of those listening—surprise, disbelief, interest. Three years ago, I was afraid to speak. Could I be honest, even with myself, and risk appearing foolish?

"I don't know, Ami, but Doctor Luke and I are going to find out. I've never met anyone like Yeshua."

"Fair enough," Ami said.

"Where is Doctor Luke?" I asked.

Levi lifted his cane. "I believe he went to Caesarea."

I'd probably miss him on this trip. I wouldn't be here that long. After a few more minutes of drabble, I finished eating and returned to my room.

Before lying down, I wrote two pages of copious notes. I wanted Dr. Luke to have a first-hand account of what had transpired over the last day. I was also anxious to examine the scrolls in Mr. Snyder's extensive collection. Perhaps after having read those documents, I would understand more.

I pulled out the sealed scroll from the temple. The golden nugget fell out also. Would I ever be able to open the parchment? I should have asked Shale where the golden nugget came from—or had she told me and I forgot? I massaged my aching head.

❋

Sometime in the late evening, I fell asleep. Unfamiliar noises startled me and I opened my eyes. The oil lamp had burned out. A cold draft—as icy cold as in the cave—filled the darkened room. When my eyes adjusted, I realized several hooded beings stood around my bed. Animal-like noises came from them.

I brandished my arm through the air to shoo them away. I tried to sit up, but I was too weak from sleep—as if drugged.

The creatures backed away from the bed, but I sensed they wanted something.

"Get out of here!" I shouted.

One of the creatures pointed at me with a leathery, black finger, as if burned by fire. "Give me the scroll."

I clasped the scroll underneath my body and pulled myself up. "No. It's sealed."

"Take it," another one said.

One of the creatures swung at me with a long heavy object. I dodged out of the way. Before he tried again, a deep guttural roar filled the room. The hooded creatures froze. Seconds later, they hissed and flew out of the locked door—without opening it.

A lion stood across from me. Superimposed over him was a lamb that dripped with blood.

The lion spoke. "The scroll must stay in your possession."

As I studied the image of both animals, they faded away.

I couldn't get my breath. I jumped out of bed and struggled to light the lamp with my shaky hand. I paced back and forth. The hooded creatures must have been demons, but who was the lion? I picked up my shredded notes from the floor. Who did this? And why did the demons want the scroll?

After a few minutes, I calmed down. The lion had appeared to me three times and the bloodied lamb twice. I climbed back into bed. I would need to rewrite everything.

I realized something else. The lion had scared the demons away. Were he and Yeshua the same? What about the lamb? Were all three the same?

I'd write my notes a hundred times if I had to. Few people outside of the council knew the details. I wouldn't let a few demons frighten me.

CHAPTER 35

When I left for Galilee, the roads were still crowded. Many folks appeared edgy as gossip circulated. Galilee had been Yeshua's headquarters. What would happen to the rabbi's followers? Would those associated with him be shunned—or even excommunicated from the synagogue?

Rumors of an empty tomb were even more disturbing. Did the disciples steal Yeshua's body? Had the rabbi come back to life? Speculation was rampant.

Almost two weeks after leaving Jerusalem, I arrived at Brutus Snyder's estate. Rains had been plentiful, and the fields around the home were a vibrant green. Fewer sheep grazed on the lush fields compared to when I lived here.

I dismounted Baruch and led him around to the back. Where was everybody?

Lowly, Shale's pig, slogged up to the wooden fence. Now was a good time to keep my promise—before I got busy and forgot. I approached the wooden railing. I had never spoken to a pig before.

I began by saying, "Shale wanted me to tell you she will miss you, but she needed to return home. She also wanted you to remember the king loves you, and she loves you, too, and will miss you deeply."

The pig made some disgusting pig sounds and wiggled his curly tail.

All right. I did it, as I promised. I should congratulate myself.

Someone laughed.

I turned. Judd was leaning against a tree.

My face grew hot. "It's rude to sneak up on people."

Judd cocked his head. "A Jew talking to a pig. That's pretty funny."

I glared at him. I never liked Judd and I disliked him now even more. "So you are still a scumbag, huh?"

Judd squinted. "What's that?"

I glared at him. "A lowlife."

"A what?"

What did they call jerks in the first century? I threw up my hands. "I have things I need to do here, and they don't include talking to you."

I tied Baruch to a post and stomped towards the house. Judd stepped in front of me.

"Excuse me, but you are in my way."

Judd didn't budge.

I started to sidestep him, but he blocked me.

"Would you please move," I demanded.

Judd put his hand on my shoulder.

I reached up but he stopped me.

"Daniel, can we talk?"

I smirked. "You are the last person I want to talk to." I shoved him. "Get out of my way."

Judd ran in front and blocked the door. "Daniel, I'm sorry, all right? I didn't know you'd get so mad at my poor joke."

I wiped the sweat from my brow. I had embarrassed Mark and he forgave me. I should give Judd some slack.

"Are you going to let me by?"

Judd shrugged. "Can we go into the stable and talk first?"

I hesitated. "What do you want to talk about?"

Judd glanced at the window. "Scylla—I need to tell you some things."

"Scylla?" What could Judd possibly need to tell me about Shale's stepmother? I had hoped to scuttle in, get Shale's diary, procure the scrolls I wanted from the library, and scuttle out. I'd also hoped to visit with Mari, the governess. Where was she anyway?

"All right. But let's make this quick."

Judd plodded over to the post to get Baruch and led him into the cave. He didn't say anything else until after he gave the donkey some oats and fresh water.

I sat at the table where Shale and I had talked when we first met. Nothing had changed except Assassin, Judd's donkey, wasn't in his pen.

A few minutes later, Judd came over and joined me. He stretched his hand across the table.

I shook my head. "No."

Judd pulled his hand away and leaned back in the chair. "I don't know where to start."

"Why don't you begin with Scylla."

"All right. The Romans blasted in here a few days ago—searching for you. They roughed up Scylla. When they left, she locked herself in the room. Mari got away before the Romans touched her. The soldiers let all the animals loose and threatened to kill me if I didn't tell them where you were. Of course, I didn't know."

I swallowed hard. "Where did Mari go?"

"I don't know, but a young woman was here a couple of weeks ago. Mari might have gone to warn her."

"Cynisca?"

Judd squinted. "I don't remember her name, but she had horses and needed a place to stay. She said you sent her."

"Do you know how to find Mari?"

Judd shrugged "I thought Mari would be back by now. I'm concerned that's she's not."

"What did the Romans do to Scylla?"

Judd shook his head.

I glanced away feeling uncomfortable. Mr. Snyder's wife had bullied everyone. How could I feel compassion for her, of all people?

Judd scooted his chair closer to the table. "There is more."

"What?"

He leaned towards me. "I'm a follower of Yeshua."

"What?" My voice cracked.

Judd threw up his hands. "I decided to follow his teachings. I recognized my rebellion and wanted to change."

"Did you know he died in Jerusalem over Pesach?"

Judd's eyes grew wide. "What?"

I explained what happened to the teacher, going into more detail than I had intended, but Judd listened with such interest I talked for the better part of an hour.

When I stopped, Judd reached across the table again. I shook his hand this time. There was peace between us—for the moment.

"So, Judd, what should we do?"

He tapped his fingers. "I found most of the animals along the road —except for my donkey and some of the sheep. The Romans didn't bother with the pigs. I cleaned up the place. Scylla hasn't come out of her room since they left."

I crossed my arms. "I probably don't have time to help you look for the sheep, but if Scylla hasn't come out of her room, how do you know she is even in there?"

"She comes out at night and takes food back to her room. We weren't speaking even before the soldiers came."

"Why?"

"We had a falling out after I started following Yeshua. She thinks I betrayed her."

"How could you have betrayed her?"

Judd shrugged. "It's a long story. I wanted out of the agreements. When I became a follower of Yeshua, God showed me my dishonesty. I had hurt Shale."

"What happened with the betrothal?"

Judd shook his head. "I voided the contract. It was about the dowry."

"You realized this when you became a follower of Yeshua?"

Judd nodded. "He changed me. And now you say he's dead."

"Rumors are he's alive."

Judd shook his head. "Can't be."

"What can't be?"

Judd stared into space. "Just things he said."

I twitched my neck. "Like what?"

"He said he would rise on the third day."

"Did you hear him say this?"

Judd was silent for a moment. "Either I heard him say it or someone told me he said it. I can't remember now."

We chitchatted a few more minutes when Judd asked, "So, why did you come back?"

I had almost forgotten. "I came to get Shale's diary. She forgot it and wants me to send it to her."

"So she did return home?"

"You didn't know?"

Judd tapped his fingers again. "She left without telling anyone. Not even Mari, which wasn't like her."

"Maybe she was afraid you might stop her."

"I thought she might have gone to her father—or you. We were all worried, but the Romans came the next day. Her sudden departure was a blessing."

I reflected on Judd's words.

He interrupted my thoughts. "You can check Shale's room, but you shouldn't let Scylla know you're here. She'll blame you for the attack. She's—not stable."

"Can we go now? And can you keep an eye out for Scylla?"

"Yes. Let's go."

CHAPTER 36

W e crossed the stone portico nestled behind the kitchen. Early blooming flowers bordered the edges and decorated the trellis. I imagined Mari sticking her head out of the kitchen door to greet us.

I glanced across the field, remembering. Shale always wanted to tell me about the king, as she referred to him. I rejected him—and rejected her in the process.

Judd brought me back to reality when he slammed into me.

"Sorry, Daniel."

"My fault, I was daydreaming."

"I don't think Scylla will come out of her room during daylight. She's terrified of the soldiers returning."

"You are sure she's alive?"

"Oh, yeah. As I said, she's leaving half-eaten food in the kitchen. Mari left a few days ago, and no one else is here."

"You're sure Mari will be back?"

Judd replied. "She'll be back."

How could he be sure?

Judd tapped me on the shoulder. "Go. If Scylla appears, I'll detain her. When you're done, return to the cave through the field. I'll meet you in twenty minutes. Is that enough time?"

"Should be." I hurried to Shale's quarters. When I opened the door, the room was empty. The only thing I saw was a stripped-down bed and an empty chest. I examined inside the drawers, under the rugs—there was no evidence she had ever been here.

Did Mari clean her room? I checked the night table and chest again and searched under her bed. All Shale's belongings were gone. Frustrated, I went back to the cave. A few minutes later, Judd returned.

"Did you find the scrolls?"

"No. Someone cleaned out the room."

Judd shook his head. "Strange. Either Scylla took the scrolls or Mari took them."

"We'll need to check Scylla's room."

Judd frowned. "How?"

I pressed my elbows into the table "Suppose we tear down the door?"

"Are you serious?"

"I promised Shale I would get them for her—preferably before Scylla took them."

Judd groaned. "Can we think about it for a day or two?"

Was Judd telling the truth? Suppose he had the diary? Did he murder Scylla and Mari? I rubbed the back of my neck, stalling. Could Judd be setting me up?

I relented. "I suppose waiting a day or two won't make any difference. Let's talk more tomorrow."

Judd crossed his arms. "Perhaps you should stay here. I'll bring you some blankets."

"All right." If he was a follower of Yeshua, as he claimed to be, I had no reason to doubt him—did I?

The next morning, Judd brought me figs and bread. While I ate, he fed the animals and watered them. He gave extra feed to Lowly, Shale's pig, and Baruch. His work ethic was more diligent than before.

After he finished, he sat beside me at the table.

Did Yeshua make that much of a difference in his life? "Tell me, who do you believe Yeshua is—or was?"

Judd whistled under his breath. "The Son of God, the Messiah."

He repositioned himself in the chair. "If he has risen, he would have to be. No human can come back from the dead."

"But what would be the point? Why die and come back to life?"

Judd winced. "Why do you sacrifice animals?"

I hesitated. "To make ourselves right with God."

Judd waved his hand. "In other words, to make atonement for your transgressions."

I nodded. "Yes, that's what I mean."

Judd scooted closer. "John the Baptist said of Yeshua, 'Behold, the Lamb of God, who takes away the sins of the world."

"John the Baptist said that?"

"Yes, before Herod beheaded him." Judd leaned back in his chair. "Someone told me Yeshua said he was the resurrection and the life. He wouldn't have said that if he wasn't predicting his death. If what you say is true—some have seen him alive—that would mean many prophecies have been fulfilled."

I could no longer avoid the question. What if many had been mistaken for two thousand years? My hands began to shake.

Judd reached over, "Are you all right?"

"Yes." I stood. "I need some fresh air. I'll be back."

I stumbled out of the cave, opened the gate, and ran out to the field. The luscious grass and crisp air invigorated me. Birds chirped from the trees. I laid down where Shale and I used to talk, closed my eyes, and tried to remember our conversations.

I remembered the picture she drew of a man battling a demon. When I mocked her drawing, she scooted up on her knees and pleaded. "Don't waste this opportunity, Daniel. We don't always have second opportunities in life to do the important things. It's too easy to squander what matters."

I didn't have a second chance with Shale. I lost my opportunity to be with her and to share what was most important in her life.

Who was Yeshua? If the rabbi wasn't the Messiah, how did he bring the young girl back to life? How did he heal the lepers? How did he raise Lazarus from the dead? The rabbi once said, "If you don't believe in me, believe in the works I do."

How did I explain the train ride to Auschwitz, the dog that rescued me in the temple, the provision of the horse from Solomon's stables, the Nazi apparitions, the earthquake when Yeshua died, the darkening of the sky when he passed, and the strange resurrection of the grave people? Perhaps Pilate asked Yeshua the most important question—what is truth?

The ventriloquist—she misled me. She encouraged me to do evil. She pursued me everywhere—from Dothan to Galilee to Caesarea to Jerusalem and back to Dothan. Why?

The demons wanted to kill me for the scroll. The lion saved my life.

I rubbed my eyes. I even remembered the angels who rescued me when the chariot flipped. Was there a connection between losing my contacts in the accident and the times when everything turned gray?

I bowed my head and prayed, "YHWH, please show me if Yeshua is the Messiah. Is he your son, the son of David?"

I didn't care about anything except knowing the truth, but God didn't answer me.

I prayed again. "Have mercy on me, Lord, I'm a stupid man. Please show me if Yeshua is the Messiah."

Several hours passed, and the sun lowered in the sky. I did nothing but commune with God. At last, I got up and returned to the cave. Judd sat at the table. Was he still waiting for me? I walked over to the water jug and washed my face. After I composed myself, I sat beside him.

He spoke first. "Would you like to go to the Sea of Galilee tomorrow? We need to figure out how to get into Scylla's room. And who knows, maybe Mari will be back."

"You are sure she'll be back?"

Judd assured me again. "She'll be back."

"All right. Thanks—for everything."

Judd smiled. "Yeshua changed my life."

I swallowed hard.

He reached out, and I shook his hand. "I'll bring you some more food. And get some sleep."

CHAPTER 37

The next morning, when Judd came over to feed the animals, I helped him as I used to. "Any sign of Mari?"

Judd gave Baruch a large bucket of fresh water. "No, not yet."

"Did you see Scylla?"

Judd shook his head. "Her door is still shut. And locked."

"Suppose Mari returns while we're gone? Will she be concerned you aren't here?"

Judd poured some water for the other animals. "That's a good point. I'll leave her a note."

A cloudless sky and a warm breeze made it a perfect day for traveling. Galilee, with its lush green fields and rolling hills, was especially beautiful in the spring.

I asked Judd, "Do you come to the Sea of Galilee often?"

"No, not that often. I used to come to hear Yeshua teach. I met Shale here once when I passed out bread and fish to five thousand people."

Shale never told me about that, but then talking about Judd was not a favorite topic of conversation for her. My thoughts wandered. I'd forgotten how peaceful the lake was. We paused to admire the vista from a distance. Boats on the lake created a picturesque view as nets glimmered on the water's surface. Gulls squawked overhead. A few of the birds would be lucky when the fishermen discarded what they didn't want.

I motioned at Judd. "Look at those people down there."

Judd's eyes bulged. He choked on his words. "I think—that's Yeshua."

"You think—"

Judd didn't wait to hear my question. He took off on his horse and galloped down the hill. I followed.

We tied up our horses and joined the multitude. Close to five hundred listeners sat on the grass in front of the teacher.

"It is the Lord," Judd said.

I inched closer to the front—as close as I dared. Yeshua's face shone with unspeakable joy. A supernatural luminescence surrounded the Master, erasing all suffering—the jeers, the torture, and the brutality of the crucifixion. He had defeated those who had sought to kill him. He had conquered death. No one asked who he was. Everyone knew.

I stared at the man—the perfect lamb slaughtered on Pesach. He could have saved himself—and didn't. He chose to die. His words at the cross, "Father, forgive them, for they know not what they do," would never be forgotten.

Yeshua said, "Remember the words that I have spoken to you, that there is no servant greater than his Master. If they have persecuted me, they will persecute you also."

For the first time, I believed. He was the king of the Jews, as Pontius Pilate wrote on the cross. I glanced at Judd. Yeshua's love crossed nationalities, political barriers, and stood the test of time. He was the great "I am."

There could not have been the resurrection without Yeshua's death. When he said, "It is finished," he conquered death, because even as he died, he knew he would rise again. How could Yeshua love everyone, including his enemies, so much that he was willing to suffer and die for them—unless he was God's son?

I studied the faces of those around me—from these five hundred, Christianity would spread. Born from the roots of Judiasm, all the way back to Abraham, Isaac, and Jacob, our religion gave Christianity birth. Salvation came from the Jews. Yeshua's name in Greek would become known around the world as Jesus, the Christ.

The dark forces at work since Yeshua's resurrection had blinded many. Pontius Pilate had asked the right question to the one who was truth. "What is truth?"

When I had a chance, I would check out Brutus Snyder's scrolls in the library. His collection included many writings from the Hebrew Scriptures.

I knelt, dropped my head and prayed. For the first time, I heard Yeshua's words and understood.

"For God so loved the world that he gave his only and unique son, so that everyone who trusts in him may have eternal life, instead of being utterly destroyed."

CHAPTER 38

On the way back, we discussed how to break into Scylla's quarters. However, when we arrived, we discovered Scylla's door was already open. We listened, but didn't hear any noises coming from her room. Judd motioned for me to follow him outside.

We went back to the cave, and Judd shut the door behind us.

I absent-mindedly followed the lines of the cave wall. "Do you think she's in there?"

Judd shuffled his feet. "I don't know. If you want to go in first, I'll guard the hallway—in case she tries to enter. Or I can go in and you can stand guard."

"Do you think we are making more out of this than we need to? I mean, can't we knock on the door and see if she welcomes us?"

"You didn't leave on good terms, and Scylla and I weren't speaking. We communicated through Mari. I only stayed here to take care of the animals."

I offered to enter the room first. "If she's not in there, I can search. What a blessing it would be if I found Shale's scrolls without even seeing Scylla."

"Yes, it would be," Judd agreed.

I leaned against the wall. "She's probably not in there. Why would she leave the door open when she's kept it locked until now?"

"Good point. Let's go."

I added, "I'm disappointed Mari hasn't returned."

"Yes, me too, but I feel certain she'll be back."

We returned to the house and crept quietly through the kitchen and down the hallway. I leaned over the door entrance and stuck my head inside.

Judd spoke in a low voice, "Is she in there?"

I shook my head.

Strewn clothes covered the floor and papers cluttered the desk. I glanced at her expensive furniture. Several large figurines decorated the dresser top. They reminded me of the idols in Caesarea. What god or gods did she worship? Even though they had no power, they still made me uncomfortable.

I'd check the dresser last. I scooted over to the vanity and tried to open the drawer. I jiggled it, calling out to Judd, "Do you have the keys…"

Before I could finish, out of the corner of my eye, I saw a body lunge towards me. Seconds later, a sharp object pierced my shoulder. Blood oozed followed by searing, stabbing pain.

I moaned and staggered. When I turned, Scylla faced me. Her lurid eyes betrayed passion and hate. I braced for another attack as Judd flew into the room. When he saw the bloodied knife in her hand, he stopped.

Scylla pivoted. Judd stood to the left and I was on the floor to her right. She flailed the knife wildly between us.

Judd exclaimed, "Scylla, what are you doing?"

Scylla hesitated before lunging at me again. "It's his fault," she screamed.

I touched my hand on my shoulder. Blood had seeped through my robe.

I pleaded. "Scylla, put down the knife. I'm only here to get Shale's scrolls and then I'm out of here."

Scylla let out a plaintive cry and dropped it.

Judd flew over and seized her from behind. "We need some rope to tie her up."

I moved closer and clutched the bloodied knife. Searing pain shot down my arm.

A few seconds later, Mari ran into the room. Before she could say anything, Judd yelled, "Quick, get some rope from the cave."

She took off as I sat on the floor dizzy.

"You're hurting me," Scylla groaned.

"Quit fighting," Judd demanded.

Scylla stopped squirming, and Judd pulled her over to a chair. We waited for Mari to return with the rope.

Judd glanced at me "Are you all right?"

"Yeah, I think so." I pressed on my wound to keep from losing more blood.

Mari returned a few minutes later. Judd tied Scylla's hands to the back of the chair as Mari examined my shoulder.

"Oh, my."

I rolled my eyes. "Well, how bad is it?"

"Let me clean it and bandage it," she said. "I've seen worse."

She helped me out into the kitchen, and Judd stayed with Scylla.

I started to take off the robe but she stopped me. "Let me cut if off. You shouldn't move your shoulder."

"It's the only one I brought," I protested.

"You can have one of Mr. Snyder's robes."

I acquiesced.

She cut away the clothing and wiped off the blood.

"It's not too bad, not too deep," Mari said.

Good. I'd be laid up for a few days, but other than that, I'd recover. "So what took you so long to get here?"

Mari rubbed some kind of plant salve over my injury.

"Ouch."

"Sorry, but it will help it to heal," she assured me.

I squinted. "Are you almost done?"

She nodded. "The Romans came here searching for you. They claimed you had stolen two racing horses. The animals belonged to a famous charioteer. Not only that, but the charioteer's daughter was missing."

"Cynisca. Did she come here?"

Mari smiled. "I'm getting to that."

"All right."

"Her father suspected you kidnapped her. A Roman guard on patrol claimed he saw the horses at Mr. Snyder's farm."

"I never thought this could happen."

Mari bit her lip. "I thought it would be all right to board them here for a few days until we found another place. The soldier did some checking with his superiors and made the connection you used to work here for Mr. Snyder. That implicated Mr. Snyder.

When Mr. Snyder found out, he immediately announced his intentions to divorce Scylla to disassociate himself. He claimed you no longer worked for him, he hadn't seen you in months, and Scylla must have been involved."

I took a deep breath.

Mari continued. "Shale had left before they came—but she didn't tell anyone. When this happened, we thought the worst. Do you know if she went back to her mother's?"

"Yes, she returned home."

Mari sighed, relieved. "I'm glad. I didn't think she would leave without telling me, but it was a blessing she wasn't here."

I nodded.

"Well," Mari continued, "because Mr. Snyder announced his intention of divorcing Scylla, the Romans had no respect for her. They flew in here, broke the gate, scattered the animals, and treated Scylla wrongly. They wanted to punish her, they said, for aiding in the crime."

I interrupted Mari. "Cynisca needed a place to hide. Her life was in danger."

"I know. Cynisca said you would come after Pesach. She was horrified to learn her father had brought these charges. She could only ride one horse, so to get back as quickly as possible, I rode the second horse with her to Caesarea."

"I thought she left a note for her father. Perhaps he never saw it."

"Cynisca said she fled Caesarea in the middle of the night with you because a stalker had threatened to kill her."

"Yes," I agreed.

Mari smiled. "She spoke fondly of you. Once you started racing chariots, however, you became a slave under Roman law. Why did you do such a foolish thing?"

I shrugged. "I could earn more money racing chariots than anything else."

Mari sighed. "I visited my family on the way back. My father Theophilus knew the truth. Thankfully, you and Cynisca had stopped at his place before you left Caesarea."

"I'd almost forgotten he and his wife adopted you."

"Father didn't know it had turned into treachery. He said he would do what he could to clear up your name, but the Romans have little regard for slaves—even famous ones, like you."

"How did you learn all of this?"

"I listened to the soldiers interrogating Scylla and when they talked amongst themselves. Of course, I hid, so they didn't know. And when I spoke to Cynisca, we put it together."

"You speak Latin?"

Mari smiled. "Of course. You know that. Or should have."

"You always spoke Aramaic here."

"That's just because we are in Galilee." Mari exhaled deeply. "But there is something else you don't know."

"What?"

"Something I should tell you at last."

"What?" I repeated.

Mari peered into my eyes. "I'm your half-sister."

My mind reeled. "What?"

"It is so."

"How can that be? I don't have a sister named Mari."

"Yes, you do. You don't know it because Theophilus and my mother adopted me when I was a baby, before you were born."

I stared at Mari. "Does Doctor Luke know? Did Theophilus arrange this ahead of time so we would meet?"

Judd interrupted our conversation from the other room. "Are you done in there?"

I replied, "Yes, we'll be there in a minute."

"Why didn't you tell me this before? Why the secrecy?"

"I hid my Jewishness from Brutus and Scylla. If I told you, I was afraid they would find out since you are Jewish."

"Would it have mattered, if they knew?"

"I would have had to explain too many things—things difficult to talk about. I consider Theophilus and my mother my parents. It wasn't until you arrived I realized you were my half-brother."

"But how?"

"I saw the papers for your hire. And, yes, Theophilus set this up. We talked about this when I was in Caesarea. Doctor Luke told Theophilus about you, but Theophilus didn't tell me you were my brother, in case it didn't work out. He also said he wasn't sure if I was ready to deal with the past."

I considered Mari's words and the implications. Did I have a half-sister named Mari in 2015?

Mari finished wrapping the wound. "I will need to change the bandage a couple of times each day. You should probably not lift anything."

I clasped Mari by the arm, "Can you tell Scylla I'm not guilty of any of the things the Romans accuse me of? She will believe you."

"But you did instigate some of this. You must take some responsibility."

"Not to hurt anyone. It was to protect Cynisca from a woman who had threatened her and two wicked brothers I didn't trust."

"I can try," Mari assured me.

CHAPTER 39

"Mari and I returned to Scylla's quarters. I leaned against the doorway as Mari sat beside the former Mrs. Snyder. My shoulder throbbed and I wanted to lie down, but standing would help me to stay alert. The loss of blood had fatigued me.

Scylla wept. With her hands tied, she couldn't wipe her tear-covered face. Mari took a handkerchief and dabbed the woman's eyes.

"Untie her," I said.

Judd flinched. "What?"

"She's not going to try anything with all of us here."

Judd loosened the ropes and Scylla covered her face with the handkerchief.

A healthy dose of humility had replaced Scylla's arrogance. Her indulgent, cocky mannerisms had died a painful death. Without Brutus, she had no rights, no money, and no resources. I didn't know what would happen to her.

We waited until Scylla composed herself.

I glanced at Mari. "Do you want to tell her?"

Mari nodded. With an immense tenderness, she explained what had happened. I appreciated Mari even more now knowing she was my half-sister.

When Mari finished, Scylla stared trance-like at the floor.

I broke the silence. "Scylla, I need Shale's scrolls. I promised her I would come and get them."

Scylla remained unfazed.

"Do you know where they are?"

"Yes," she admitted to us.

"Can I have them?"

Scylla waved her hand flippantly. "Even if I give them to you, you can't read them."

"What do you mean?"

"She wrote them in some sort of strange language."

I smiled on the inside. Scylla couldn't read English. "So you do have them?"

Scylla's swollen eyes beseeched me. "If I give them to you, how long will you let me stay here?"

I glanced at Judd. Was that why she locked herself in the room? Since Brutus Snyder had divorced her, she needed to leave—but she had no place to go.

Scylla had caused everyone so much grief I didn't feel sorry for her. I didn't even like her, but after watching Yeshua treat those who hated him with so much grace, I wanted to be like him. I didn't want to be the one to throw her out—even if she had tried to kill me.

Besides, I had killed a Roman guard—who was I that I should gloat over her misfortune. Still, I needed Shale's scrolls.

Judd replied, "We aren't going to throw you out of the house. I suppose Brutus might want to sell the estate, but that will take some time."

Scylla voice cracked. "The Roman soldiers said I needed to leave. I have no place to go."

Mari jumped in. "Scylla, you can stay with my friend since Cynisca left."

Scylla dabbed her eyes. "I'm afraid of the Romans. I have no protection now."

I reassured her. "If you give me the scrolls, I promise, we'll find a place for you, whether it's with Mari's friend or somewhere else. And once Mr. Snyder knows you had nothing to do with what happened, he might even change his mind."

Scylla burst into tears. "Now that Nathan is healed and with his father, Brutus has no reason to come back. He loves his wife there more than me."

I couldn't argue with the truth.

I tried again. "Scylla, if you will give me the scrolls, we can figure this out. Cynisca is back with her father now, so the Romans have no reason to be concerned with you."

Scylla acquiesced. She pointed to the objects on the dresser. "They are inside my gods."

I cringed and glanced at Judd. "You mean those tall things?"

Scylla nodded. "That's Gad, the god of fortune, the one you're holding. Turn it over. A scroll is inside it. As well as in Meni, the god of destiny, and a third scroll is in Nehushtan."

I removed the scrolls from the three idols. I should have asked Shale how many scrolls there were in all.

"Is this all of them?" I asked.

Scylla nodded.

I hesitated. Should I throw out her idols and tell her about Yeshua?

"Scylla, these gods of yours have no power, but I can tell you—"

Scylla waved her hand. "I don't believe in anything anymore. All the gods are worthless."

"Hand them to me," Judd said.

After making sure I had removed the scrolls, I gave Judd the worthless idols and he took them outside.

I needed to think of something to say—to broach the subject. "These false gods of destiny and fortune and the third one—I forgot his purpose or his name—they have deceived you. The God of Abraham, Isaac, and Jacob is different."

I continued, "Yeshua, who died on the cross a couple of weeks ago, is God's son. His death and resurrection can make your future better. He can give you peace right now despite your pain."

Scylla dabbed her eyes, but didn't say anything.

Judd returned a few minutes later. "We need to clean out this room

—there might be other things in here that could be a hindrance to her —progress."

Diplomatic, I had to admit.

"I'll be glad to help her clean up," Mari offered.

"Thank you," I replied.

Now that I had Shale's scrolls, what should we do—tie her up again?

Judd knew her better than I did. I would trust his judgment. He didn't suggest it, so I let it go.

I was tired and my shoulder hurt, but I was thankful. Judd and I left the women and walked outside. Darkness was approaching.

I rubbed my chin. "I need to shave."

Judd stared at me. "You do?"

"What can I use?"

Judd chuckled. "Scylla's knife."

I threw up my hands. "Are you serious?"

CHAPTER 40

I spent the next few days reading Shale's diary in Brutus Snyder's library. When I spread the scrolls out on top of his desk, fond memories returned. I had taught Nathan, Shale's half-brother, how to read here.

Shale's knowledge and understanding of spiritual things was much superior to mine. It took me a while to figure out why her entries began with "Dear Dog." So like Shale, to add a bit of humor. Dog was God spelled backwards.

Because of Shale's conflict with her father and stepmother, her diary had become like a prayer journal. In one place, she wrote, "Why can't I be Jewish?"

Even with Jewish persecution throughout history, she perceived that the Jewish people held a special place in Yeshua's heart. The rabbi spent most of his time among the Jews as a Jew himself. Why wouldn't the Jews be God's chosen people?

I unrolled the scroll. "Dear Dog, you must have a sense of humor. Who else would send me back in time to meet a rabbit, a dog, a pig, and a donkey—in a land where a powerful king roams like a pauper, and a handsome young man has smitten me with love?"

I closed my eyes and imagined her penning these words. She

recorded this entry soon after she arrived. I unrolled the scroll a bit more, but I didn't see where she mentioned me again.

In another place, I found, "He makes the blind see and the deaf hear, just like he healed my brother." A hand-drawn heart highlighted Nathan's name.

I set Shale's scrolls aside. Tears filled my eyes and I had to stop reading. I searched for other scrolls in Mr. Snyder's collection. The one of Joel caught my eye. On the few occasions we went to the synagogue, I never heard the rabbi read from the prophets.

I put the scroll of Joel back and pulled out the scroll of Daniel. I unrolled it to the end and found the paragraph that had intrigued me.

> At that time, Michael, the great commander, will
> stand up on behalf of the descendants of your
> people. It will be a time of trouble unlike any
> that has existed from the time there have
> been nations until that time. But at that time
> your people, everyone written in the book,
> will be rescued. Many sleeping in the ground
> will wake up. Some will wake up to live
> forever, but others will wake up to be
> ashamed and disgraced forever. Those who
> are wise will shine like the brightness on the
> horizon. Those who lead many people to
> righteousness will shine like the stars forever
> and ever.
> But you, Daniel, keep these words secret, and
> seal the book until the end times. Many will
> travel everywhere, and knowledge will grow.

Dr. Luke had shown me this passage. What scroll did Michael, the protector of Israel, mean? And what were the end times? I returned the scroll to the shelf.

The more I read, the more I wanted to read. David's Psalms presented many questions. King David indicated in one place that the

Messiah would suffer what appeared to be death by crucifixion—before crucifixion had been invented, writing that the Messiah's hands and his feet would be pierced.

In another place, King David predicted men would gamble for the Messiah's clothing. He prophesized that the Messiah would be accused by false witnesses, hated without a cause, and betrayed by a friend. David, the Psalmist, even hinted at the Messiah's resurrection.

I sat back and admired the scrolls. I doubted Mr. Snyder appreciated the vast treasure trove hidden in his personal library. These scrolls would be priceless in 2015. How wrong would it be if I borrowed the books of Joel and Daniel—to preserve history?

I wanted to keep reading but a more pressing matter nudged me. How could I get Shale's scrolls to her? I knew of one place where her writings would be safe for two thousand years.

If only I could return home, but I hadn't met any angels. If I hid them amongst the Dead Sea Scrolls, a scientist might find them—with lots of questions that would make news headlines. I chuckled, imagining the discussion that would follow among scholars.

Mari interrupted my musings when she walked into the library. "How is your shoulder?"

I moved my arm. "It only hurts when I use it."

"Here." Mari manipulated my arm gently.

I groaned.

"If you don't stretch it, you'll end up with a frozen shoulder."

I submitted to the painful therapy. "How is Scylla?"

Mari smiled. "We cleaned up her room. She's much better now."

"Did you hide the knives?"

Mari put my arm down. "She's sorry for what she did to you."

"Yeah, me, too. At least I have plenty of reading material."

"When are you leaving?"

"As soon as my shoulder is healed."

"Will you be going to Caesarea?"

"No—Ein Gedi."

Mari's eyes twinkled. "Judd told me his betrothal to Shale is no longer."

I nodded. "Yes, Judd told me also."

"And I see you're reading Shale's diary."

I smiled. "Yes, with great interest."

"Shale loves you."

"So you think I should propose to her?"

Mari rolled her yes. "Don't let her get away. While you are in Ein Gedi, you should purchase some opobalsamum perfume. She could wear it on your wedding day."

I chuckled. "Thanks for your help with Scylla and Shale. You've been a huge blessing."

"I'm sure God meant it to be."

An idea occurred to me. "I promised Theophilus I would return to Caesarea and give him my full accounting of Yeshua. I'd love for you to come. We have much to share."

Mari smiled. "Theophilus never wanted me to forget my Jewish heritage. He fell in love with Jewish culture and hired a tutor to help me learn Hebrew."

"That helps to explain his interest in Yeshua. We must talk more before I leave."

Mari smiled. "God has used even your injury to be a blessing."

I remembered something Shale wrote in her diary. "I count it as all joy…believing you have better things for me in the future."

CHAPTER 41

I spent some time planning the trip to Ein Gedi to allow my shoulder to heal. The most grueling part of the journey would be the hike to Bethany carrying the supplies on my back. I would spend the night in Dothan—and hoped to see Dr. Luke—and leave for Bethany the next day.

That would give me time to visit with Simon, Mark, Lilly, Martha, and Mary before heading to Ein Gedi. Truth would take me the rest of the way on horseback.

I had not been to Qumran in years. Best known as the home of the Essenes, archeologists had mined the ancient ruins for clues to the past. An odd set of religious fanatics lived in the remote area to escape the trappings of the temple. Many claimed the fringe group hid the scrolls in the high caves facing the Dead Sea.

Their writings revealed they had abandoned the temple culture. Having witnessed the council's corruption, I didn't blame them. My new appreciation and understanding of the times when Yeshua lived enhanced my empathy for the factions that struggled to survive.

No one knew what happened to the curious group. Perhaps when Masada fell, the Romans slaughtered them—or they committed suicide as their Jewish brothers did to avoid capture.

Mari mentioned that an inn near the oasis of Ein Gedi was the best place to stay. The romantic waterfall, luscious plants, and native wildlife of Ein Gedi near Qumran created an oasis in an area otherwise devoid of life.

I had sealed Shale's scrolls in jars similar to those the Essenes used. Perhaps the trickiest part would be to sneak past the community near the cliff caves. I didn't want a confrontation with the religious sect. They were too well-known for their eccentricity and exclusivity.

I rubbed my naked chin. The change in my appearance surprised me. Mari had also cut my hair. No Roman would ever recognize me. I loved the freedom anonymity would give me—a welcome reprieve from my constant fear of recapture.

A week later, I left Galilee. The Pesach crowds had dissipated, and the roads were wide open. After walking for a day, I stopped in Dothan for the night.

Ami and Levi didn't recognize me. "You don't even look like a Jew," Ami said.

"That's great," I replied. "I can travel like a Roman."

Dr. Luke had not returned from Caesarea—at least that's where Ami and Levi thought he went—so I was disappointed we didn't have an opportunity to talk.

The next day I left Dothan and passed through Jerusalem to Bethany. The effects of the quake were still visible although life appeared to have returned to normal. The extra Roman garrisons brought in for the festival had cleared out.

I imagined Pontius Pilate happily back in Caesarea after a very stressful visit to Jerusalem. History would never figure out the compli- cated man. I was glad I wasn't him.

I traveled through Jerusalem and Bethphage without stopping and made it to Bethany in good time.

No one recognized me when I knocked on the door—not even Mark.

"I want to shave, too," he said.

I laughed. He had hardly anything on his chin worth shaving.

Martha and Mary prepared a meal of fish and bread, and Simon and I reclined at the table discussing the events of the last few weeks.

"A sense of uneasiness has settled over Jerusalem," Simon remarked, "since the death of Yeshua."

"Like what?" I asked.

"Fear of persecution. Peter has stepped forward as the new leader. The good news is Yeshua has been seen by the disciples and many others."

I rejoiced I could share my story with the former leper. "I saw him in Galilee with about five hundred people."

Simon replied, "Yes, we heard. His appearances have shocked the believers, but did he not predict he would die and be resurrected?"

I pointed towards the table where Yeshua had reclined. "I heard him predict it right here the night before going to Jerusalem. He said of the woman who washed his feet, "She is doing this in preparation for my burial."

Simon leaned back. "Indeed. Small groups of believers are meeting in homes across Jerusalem. Those who have seen him alive are spreading the news. Of course, the council is telling everyone the disciples stole his body."

I waved my hand. "Don't listen to them. The Messiah has risen."

Simon smiled. "I prayed for you when I returned from Caesarea. Seeing you racing chariots among the heathen caused me much consternation. God answered my prayers. I'm glad you are with us now."

"If not for you, I wouldn't be here."

Simon reflected. "The Lord sent me to you. Yeshua told us, if you have the faith of a mustard seed, you can move mountains."

I reached over and clasped my long-time friend on the shoulder. "No matter what happens, no matter what anyone says, no matter how much you suffer, don't ever doubt that Yeshua is the Messiah."

Simon nodded. "You sound like a prophet."

I dropped my hand and sighed. "I will be praying for you and the others."

"Pray we will be willing to die if we must."

"I will," I promised.

Later in the afternoon, before leaving for Ein Gedi, Lilly stopped by.

"I'm glad you are now a follower of Yeshua," she whispered as she hugged me.

"You are a big reason why."

The camaraderie among the few who knew Yeshua as the Messiah was sweet. Remembering what the world was like in 2015, I would miss that connectedness. Who among my Jewish friends would listen to me? Who would believe me?

For a Jew to believe Yeshua was the long-awaited Messiah was almost impossible. What would my family think? My mother might insist I had lost my mind again and try to send me back to the Family and Youth Treatment Center. God forbid.

After saying good-bye, Truth and I continued on Robber's Road to Jericho and south through the Judean Wilderness. I contemplated the difficult terrain of the high cliffs—the biggest challenge to hiding the scrolls. I could easily carry my supplies on my back and gallop on a horse, but would my injured shoulder be strong enough to rappel up and down the steep cliffs?

I arrived at Trader's Inn in Qumran by nightfall. I checked into a room and strolled back outside. The area was desolate. The land was as dry and barren as Galilee was green and lush. Nothing worth eating even lived in the Dead Sea to the east.

After a few reflective moments, I returned to my room, anxious for the morning to arrive. I double checked my backpack. I had the jars containing Shale's scrolls, about sixty meters of rope for rappelling, gloves that belonged to Mr. Snyder, boots that belonged to Judd, some makeshift anchors, and something akin to a harness. It was actually more like a diaper, but traditional rappelling equipment didn't exist in the first century. I'd had to jerry-rig everything.

Now that I was here, I found it hard to relax. After eating a light meal and praying, I blew out the oil lamp and tried to sleep, but uncertainty consumed me—which was not conducive to a good night's rest. I didn't want the parchments found too soon. The Bedouins discovered most of the scrolls in the late 1940s and early 1950s. Many of them weren't examined in depth by experts, however, until decades later.

If only I knew how to return to 2015, I would keep them with me, but what if I never made it back?

I had weighed the pros and cons of hiding them in a cave. In the end, I always came to the same conclusion. Our apartment had been in the family for generations so if the authorities discovered the scrolls earlier than I anticipated, they knew where to find us. At the very least, they would contact us to sort out the strange writings found among the others.

I arose from a light slumber at the first rays of sunshine. After a quick bite to eat and tending to Truth's needs, I mounted the white horse in great anticipation. The mountains beckoned me. The air was cool before the noonday sun bore down and made it unbearably hot.

Years had passed since I had trekked across the desert or hiked among the cliffs. As we galloped westward, I saw the huts of those I presumed to be the Essenes.

The small shelters reminded me of a wilderness campground. I had imagined a small community or village, but perhaps the community developed later—or had already died out. My fears of a confrontation were unfounded. This early in the morning, no one was around.

Truth and I stopped in front of a rugged mountain facing the Dead Sea. I searched for a cave that looked accessible. Assuming I made it up to the cave without breaking my neck and hid Shale's scrolls, even if I wasn't able to retrieve them myself, a Bedouin or an archeological team would find them. I wrote my name and address on the jars, as well as my father's name and his father's name, in English and Hebrew. I even added Shale's contact information.

I took the rope and nails out of my backpack and studied the jagged edges of the cliff. The top of the cliff was a long ways up. The steep rock face was more severe than I imagined.

On closer inspection, slight indentations appeared evenly spaced, as if someone had already created footholds along the mountain's side. What great luck—or providence of God.

If used with great care, the indentations would provide an easier way to get to the largest of the cave entrances high overhead. I took a deep breath. While I wore boots, they weren't designed for rock-climbing and my shoulder still lacked full range of motion.

I leaned against the rocky cliff and prayed. After inspecting the best approach, I proceeded. I hammered in nails with a makeshift hammer as I climbed. I tied the rope into the nails as I proceeded and anchored the rope to me with a harness. The extra equipment was cumbersome, but gave me added protection in case I slipped or fell.

I stopped every few minutes to hydrate and rest. After nearly an hour, I reached the first of many cave entrances. I stuck my head in to see what was inside.

The morning sunshine pierced the darkness only a couple of meters. I walked as far back as the light penetrated. Once my eyes adjusted, horizontal cuts appeared in the cave wall creating a natural shelf where scrolls could be stored.

I was surprised I didn't find any scrolls because the cuts looked manmade. It could be the Essenes didn't hide them in the caves until the desperate days of Masada, or maybe I didn't see them in the low-level light.

The time of decision had arrived. I pulled out the three jars that held Shale's scrolls. I wrote on each of the jars, "followers of Yeshua" in Hebrew and English.

I wanted the jars identified differently from the others. I prayed they would be here when I came to get them—in 2015. That would mean I had made it back home.

I noticed by coincidence one of the shelves had a hidden compart-ment behind it—supernaturally it popped out as I set two jars on the shelf. How strange. For a second, I perceived another being beside me, as if someone were helping me that I couldn't see. How else could something like that happen—something beyond an ordinary explanation? Surely, even though things were not as they appeared, something existed that made the supernatural real.

After seeing Yeshua at the Sea of Galilee, could I ever doubt the presence of angels? Maybe this was what God had sent me to do—to preserve Shale's scrolls for the future as well as the scroll of Daniel I found in the temple.

I pushed the jars behind the movable wall and sealed it shut. The additional protection from the elements would help to preserve them until someone removed the scrolls—hopefully me.

Having hidden the jars, I was anxious to return to Dothan. I hoped Dr. Luke would be back. I had much I wanted to share with him. To be extra cautious, I hammered some more nails into the bedrock of the cliff, looped the rope around them, and doubled-looped the rope to my waist. After risking so much to climb up here, I didn't want to slip or fall.

The climb down was faster than the climb up until I reached the halfway point. Suddenly, an unexpected gust of wind sheared across the cliff. I lost my footing and fell. Death was only inches away as I dangled precariously off the cliff. To see the world upside down as I swayed back and forth sixty meters above the ground was terrifying.

After several failed attempts, I succeeded in getting myself upright. I pulled myself up the rope and was able to ease myself towards the cliff, enabling me to rappel but with great difficulty.

When I reached a step-up point, I clawed my way over the ledge. Exhausted, I laid there, staring up at the sky.

Only when my boots firmly touched the dirt beneath the cliff did I feel safe.

The hot desert sun was merciless, and I was thankful to be alive. The climb up had been a more grueling adventure than I had anticipated. My shoulder throbbed, but things could have turned out much worse.

Truth stood waiting patiently for me in the shade. I greeted him warmly and ran my hand along his neck. My unexpected confrontation with death reminded me of the tenuousness of life. I needed to be thankful for the life God had given me here.

I shared some of my water with Truth before galloping back to the inn. Once the air cooled, we'd head back to Dothan—mission accomplished.

CHAPTER 42

As the sun dropped behind the rocky cliffs of the Judean desert, Truth and I galloped away from Trader's Inn. Wispy clouds gathered over the wilderness and temperatures felt balmy after the heat of the noonday sun. The pink-tinted rocks covering the area west of the Dead Sea made sunsets temptingly alluring, but we needed to make it to Bethany before nightfall.

Mari had given me money for two nights, but I hated to waste it. I had also purchased some opobalsamum perfume. The fragrance possessed a mystical quality. I imagined Shale's beaming smile when I gave it to her, even indulging myself the dreamy thought of her wearing it on our wedding day.

Quite unexpectedly, I felt sad. Now that I no longer had Shale's scrolls, loneliness seeped into my soul. Suppose I never made it back? I reached into my bag and clutched the golden nugget—the only thing I had now that belonged to Shale.

I forced myself to think differently. I could always give the opobalsamum perfume to Mari—for all she had done to help me. I reached forward and patted Truth on the neck. I didn't have to be a slave to my feelings. I chose instead to thank God for his blessings.

As we galloped passed the Dead Sea, I noticed something strange. I directed Truth to turn east. As we approached the sea, sharp rocks from the salty water covered the shoreline. Truth risked cutting his hoofs on the razor-laced crystals. I nudged him gently along, but I was curious why someone would be fishing.

A man stood on the edge of the water. He held a hand-made pole with a line dangling into the water. He didn't seem to notice my approach. Did he not know there were no fish in the Dead Sea? Everyone knew that.

I called out to him. "Sir, you may be fishing a long time here. There are no fish in these waters."

He didn't respond. Could he not hear me? I came closer and started to repeat myself when he finally turned and faced me. I stared in horror.

He wasn't a man, but some sort of strange creature. His fiery eyes in his oversized sinking eye sockets spewed out flames. He held a cigarette in his deformed mouth and he had no nose—only a hole where one should have been. The creature's dark, leathery skin reminded me of a burnt marshmallow. His features barely resembled a human face.

He laughed, as if I were sport to him.

Fear welled up inside of me. The fiend's ragged clothes had concealed his identity. He had deliberately lured me in—to taunt me. Truth whinnied and lurched backwards on the sharp rocks. I dug my heels into his hindquarters, praying he wouldn't throw me off.

Within seconds, Truth bolted from the Dead Sea, and I gripped the reins tightly. Pain shot through my shoulder. Why had I come so close? I smelled sulfur.

As Truth galloped away, I never turned to glance behind me. I should have known better. I'd seen too much wickedness here. On the other hand, I had also seen much good. In the end, I knew who won.

Once we were away from the Dead Sea, my nerves calmed down. I wanted to find a place in Jericho to spend the night.

Rappelling off the cliffs had been exhausting and I needed to rest my shoulder. The throbbing pain was worse now than it had ever been, even when Scylla stabbed me.

In addition, despite my self-proclaimed bravado, after seeing the strange creature, I didn't want to travel on the road so close to dusk—especially on the road from Jericho to Jerusalem.

CHAPTER 43

The vibrant green hills around Jericho contrasted starkly to the desert area to the south and the desolate mountains to the west. The steep climb on the corkscrew road up the rugged range afforded spectacular vistas. Only Bedouins made their homes here. Nomads could live anywhere.

Remote sections of the road caused travelers great consternation. I would be glad when I arrived safely in Bethany. I hoped to make a quick stop there before continuing to Dothan. Truth would probably need the rest. The ascent could make even a hardy horse tired.

The sun had risen from the east and the trip began with little pretense of anything extraordinary. My shoulder felt better after a good night's sleep and I anticipated arriving at Dothan by sunset. I passed only two travelers on the winding road.

Life seemed to have returned to normal, at least a semblance of it, but in reality, nothing would ever be the same. The Messiah had come and brought salvation, but few recognized his appearance. The beginnings of Christianity were taking root right here among the Jews.

We traveled through a narrow slit in a mountain pass where the Romans were widening a gap. Rome's vast empire fueled its obsession with road construction. How else could they control their subjects if they didn't have access to their occupied lands? In some ways, their obsession with road building reminded me of 2015.

At this cut through the mountain, the left side of the road was shaded and a small patch of grass clung tenaciously to the rocky soil. I slowed Truth down to make sure he didn't stumble on the loose dirt. Before we exited the narrow passageway, a deep guttural groan caught my attention.

"Whoa, Truth." I hesitated as I remembered the ogre. Were those human groans? If it was only an animal, I should leave it. If it was a demon—what were the chances? Fool me once, shame on you. Fool me twice, shame on me.

It was probably an animal, nothing more, and I was not about to rescue an injured animal.

When we traveled a few more meters, I heard the moan again—this time louder. I hesitated. I couldn't leave without knowing.

If someone had helped my father, maybe he would still be alive. I turned Truth around and ambled through the narrow passage. I checked along both sides of the road, but I didn't see anything until we came to the grassy patch. A body lay face down. A few meters away, a shredded moneybag lay in a heap.

"Help me," the victim cried out. "Please don't leave me here to die."

I dismounted Truth and guided the horse over to the man. The back of the man's head was bleeding. Someone had hit him with a blunt object. A robber probably sprang out from behind the rocks, knocked him down, and stole his money.

I approached the man. "Can you move?"

He lifted one of his legs, but appeared too weak to pull himself up.

"How long have you been here?"

"I don't know," he spoke in Aramaic. "Two passed me earlier but kept going."

I remembered the two hikers. They had passed me on the other side over an hour ago.

"You have a head injury," I said. "Let me get something to stop the bleeding."

I opened my bag and pulled out a couple of pieces of cloth I had brought in case I needed an arm sling for my shoulder. I gently lifted the man's head back and tied the cloth around it. I hoped the pressure would control the bleeding.

"Thank you," he said with great effort."

"Here, let me help you to sit up." I gently pulled him up from the back, underneath his arms, and leaned him against the rock. When I saw his face, I nearly fainted. It couldn't be.

"What is your name?" I asked the man.

"Nidal Naser," the man replied.

I stared at him. His face had multiple cuts and he had a serious head injury. I didn't know if he had any broken bones, but if I didn't take care of him, he would die. He was in no condition to walk.

I forced myself to check his arm. Did he have the Yeti tattoo?

"Hold on a minute," I said.

I walked several meters away. Truth came up and nudged me from behind. I snatched the reins and buried my head in his side. I could gallop away and leave him. I had put a cloth around his head to stop the bleeding. He might recover enough to make it to Jericho. That wouldn't require him to climb too many hills; it was mostly a descent going east.

Unexpected anger filled me. I couldn't deny it or push it way. Nidal Naser had stolen my money—money I had worked three long years to earn. He was a robber. He deserved what he got. Why should I do anything to help him?

I hated him. He had ruined my life. From that day forward, I had almost lost hope of attending medical school. He not only stole my money, he stole my dreams. I used to have all the money I needed. I didn't have to worry about where my next meal would come from.

Moreover, I had been generous with everything I earned. I didn't waste it or squander it. I saved it. Why should I have mercy on him? No, there was no way I was going to help him.

My anger went deeper than Nidal Naser. I was angry with God.

I stared straight ahead. "Why, God? Why him? I'd be willing to help anyone but him. This isn't fair! You have set me up for failure.

You know I would be willing to help anybody but him—anybody but him. This is your doing, God. Why him?"

The man moaned again. I could not look at him. He was repulsive to me. I hated him, but I couldn't bring myself to mount Truth and gallop away.

I heard a voice in my head remind me, "What would Yeshua do?"

I buried my head in Truth's thick mane. Seconds ticked away as I lamented my choice. No matter how hard I tried to rationalize my right to leave him there to die, a voice inside refused to give me permission.

"Please, God," I cried in a whisper, "I'll do anything you want me to do but rescue this thief. Please don't ask me to do that."

The wind blew but no other sound spoke supernaturally to me. Not even an insect buzzed. The area was too remote.

The chances that someone else would stumble upon him were nil. He probably wouldn't live much longer without immediate help.

"I'm thirsty," the man cried out.

The way he said it reminded me of someone else who spoke those words. I clutched Truth's mane between my fingers and squeezed. I couldn't hold back the sobs. I had not the strength to help him or the guts to leave him, but I did have one thing Yeshua had given me—the ability to love. Yeshua's love for those who hated him, even as he died on the cross, convicted me.

How could I refuse to help someone whom God clearly intended for me to help? Had Yeshua not died for all men? Even me? If I left this man to die, believing Yeshua was the Messiah, what kind of man was I? Could I live with myself? How could I tell Yeshua, who died for me, "It was too hard." Was there anything too hard for God?

I lifted my head and studied Nidal. He did not recognize me without my beard. He did not know I was Daniel, the charioteer. Should I tell him? Make him feel guilty? Rub it in?

I pulled out my water bottle and returned to the helpless man. He was from the future, although I didn't know exactly when. He was stuck here, as I was. What was the reason for his visit to the first century?

How many people had visited this time and for what purpose? I had met two. Were there more? Ten, fifteen, a hundred?

I gave Yeshua water at the cross, and I would do so for Nidal—not because I wanted to, but because I had to. God's love compelled me to do what I couldn't do in my own strength.

I held Nidal's head up and allowed him to drink all the water he needed. When he finished, the jug was almost empty. I walked back to Truth and gave him the rest. I was thirsty, but they needed it more. My own thirst would remind me of Yeshua's thirst on the cross. Peace came over me. Was not love stronger than hate?

CHAPTER 44

With great difficulty, I lifted Nidal onto Truth's back. I didn't know how much farther Bethany was, but we would need to stop before continuing to Dothan. Nidal's temporary headband was bleeding through. I was anxious for Dr. Luke to check his injury.

Once we reached the top of the next mountain, Bethany appeared in the distance—not much farther. An hour later, we arrived at Simon's house. I ran in to get help.

Simon and Mark removed the nearly unconscious man from the horse as I rested my shoulder and drank several glasses of water. Once they got Nidal inside, Martha and Mary changed the bandages.

"This is a very bad head injury," Mary remarked.

"I must get him to Doctor Luke by tonight. I'll need to ride on the horse with him—if we can arrange him properly."

Simon nodded. "I can help you after you've eaten."

After a quick meal, the women packed bread, figs, dates, and nuts. Mark had taken care of Truth's needs, as always, and we took off for Dothan within the hour. Nidal seemed barely aware of his surroundings as his condition deteriorated. As much as I hated to admit it, I still struggled with rescuing him—why should I put myself out for a man I hated, except I did what God told me to do. Perhaps God would change my feelings.

We passed through Jerusalem without stopping and arrived in Dothan a few hours later. My left arm was numb from bracing Nidal against my body. My right shoulder throbbed. I was so exhausted I didn't even want to dismount the horse.

Ami and Levi were sitting on the portico with a couple of men I didn't recognize. Ami was more mobile than Levi and ran inside Jacob's Inn to get help.

Levi ambled over with his cane. A quick assessment was all he needed to recognize the urgency. "Doctor Luke returned yesterday," he said. "A good thing since this man is very ill."

"He's lost a lot of blood."

Ami returned shortly with several others. The inn had vacancies, and we carried Nidal inside and laid him down. The man opened his eyes but was unable to speak.

Dr. Luke joined us a few minutes later. After quick introductions, Dr. Luke turned his attention to his patient. "Praise God, Daniel. You saved this man's life. What happened?"

I debated how much to say. I settled on the bare facts. "I found him lying on the side of Robber's Road in a ditch. His belongings were scattered on the ground. He was robbed."

Dr. Luke washed and bandaged the head wound much more properly than I had. Nidal also had other serious injuries that needed tending.

When the doctor finished, he said, "The man needs to rest."

We walked out into the lobby, and the doctor clasped my hand and commended me on my kindness.

"So, are you staying with us for a few days?" Dr. Luke asked.

I glanced outside where new patients were waiting to be seen. "I had hoped to discuss with you the happenings in Jerusalem over the last few weeks, but you are so busy now, perhaps we should wait. I promised Mari we would travel to Caesarea to tend to business."

I wasn't ready to go into depth with Dr. Luke about our relationship.

"I just came from Caesarea," Dr. Luke replied.

Many questions filled my head. "You did?"

Dr. Luke nodded. "Theophilus sends his greetings."

"I promised Theophilus I would return and tell him more about Yeshua."

Dr. Luke added, "With the notes you wrote and what I've learned, I'm going to write a detailed account, as I promised Theophilus."

"I have no doubt it will be an excellent and trustworthy rendering," I replied.

Dr. Luke smiled and bowed slightly. "Excuse me. I need to check on another one of my patients. Being out of town the last few days has created a waiting list of people who need my attention."

"Thanks, Doctor Luke, for taking care of Nidal."

"Oh, so you know his name?" Dr. Luke asked.

"Yes," I admitted, but I wasn't ready to say how.

Dr. Luke smiled. "Excuse me." He left to tend to someone else, leaving me to lament—if I wasn't supposed to be a doctor, what did God want me to do with the rest of my life?

When I turned to leave, I saw my brother standing behind the counter. Was it really him—my brother from 2015 or Jacob Sperling from the first century? In three years, I had not seen him here.

I raised my hands and exclaimed, "Jacob!"

"Welcome to Jacob's Inn," he replied.

I glanced up at the sign. Why hadn't I made the connection? "You've never been here when I was here before. Are you the owner?"

"Of course."

I laughed and ran my hand through my hair. How could I have missed it. "I'll pick up the tab for the man I brought with me. He might be here for a few days."

Jacob nodded. "We'll figure it out. No need to worry."

I remembered when the ventriloquist told me she was my benefactor. She knew Jacob, my brother, had paid for my room. What a liar she was.

"Daniel," Jacob said, "I want to show you something."

"What?"

Jacob motioned to me. "Come closer."

What was he going to show me?

Jacob leaned over the counter and lifted his hair off his forehead. "I have the cross," he said, "as you do."

I studied his mark and touched it. Then I touched mine. "They feel the same."

"Yes," Jacob said.

"I don't even remember how it happened. How did you get yours?"

Jacob chuckled. "Soon you will know."

I didn't understand what he meant.

He pointed, "Look."

I glanced at the open door and a warm breeze drifted inside. A soft supernatural light filled the outside portico and people moved in slow motion—a clue that a door had opened.

I rushed to see. Wispy-like clouds obstructed my view. Still, my heart leaped with joy. This was the door to my future.

Forgetting everything else except the bag I never set down, I stepped through the portal and the fog instantly cleared.

CHAPTER 45

I expected to be back in Israel—in the throes of a national crisis, but instead, a magnificent garden unfolded around me. Majestic fruit trees graced the rocky walkway. Multi-colored flowers on bushes and climbing vines reached up to the canopy dripping with plump grapes.

I peered across the garden. In the distance, green undulating hills captured my imagination. I couldn't imagine a weed popping up or an annoying insect bite. The garden seemed to serve one purpose—to bring glory to the creator.

In a split nanosecond, I understood. It wasn't 2015 for which I longed. I longed for home, but not an earthly home. That would never be enough. I longed for a spiritual home, my home in the seventh dimension, the home God created just for me.

That kind of home would never be destroyed by human hands or war or evil underlings or demons.

A white rabbit hopped out of a cluster of rose bushes. Cherios—Shale's pet rabbit. She hopped towards me. Other small critters followed her.

I laughed. In my wildest dreams, I never imagined I would visit Shale's garden—or as she put it, the king's garden. I glanced around.

LORILYN ROBERTS

There must be apple trees here somewhere. I perceived the garden held many answers, but it wasn't ready to reveal its secrets.

If only I had the answer to one—why did I arrive here at the end of my journey in the seventh dimension when Shale came at the beginning of hers?

The chirping of songbirds and the splashing of a small waterfall nearby made me curious to explore. An awareness of more captivated me—more colors, more peace, more perfection, more glory.

I recognized the dog as the one from the temple. The blind cat from the nursing home came up to me and purred. Cherios, the white rabbit, stood in front of the small collection of animals. All had impacted my life in the seventh dimension.

Much-Afraid suddenly bounded in, as if she was almost late. She greeted me with her typical sashay. I reached down and petted her.

Seeing Much-Afraid raised my hopes of finding Shale here. I picked up Cherios, and she snuggled in my arms, much as she had the day she arrived with Shale at Mr. Snyder's estate.

From behind some multi-variety fruit trees, children emerged. Each one held a small kitten. I did a double take. I had seen these little ones before. They were on the train with me to Jerusalem, except they went to Auschwitz.

The illusion of time—those words popped into my head. Was it possible to be anywhere at any time in the seventh dimension? I remembered the voice I heard on the train, "Time is an illusion...."

Fear no longer overshadowed the children's faces. Their eyes radiated with joy. Exquisite robes covering their small bodies dazzled in the sunlight. The children spoke excitedly among themselves. One little boy must have been in the wrong place. An older child relocated him to the front.

The children sang a most ordinary song that brought tears to my eyes. In fact, even the ordinary was extraordinary here. I didn't know the song or recognize the words. I wasn't even sure of the language. At one moment, I thought it was Hebrew. At another, I thought it was English. Maybe it was both.

When they finished singing, I thanked them. "You have the most angelic voices. Thank you for greeting me in such a beautiful way."

One of the girls took my hand in hers She seemed familiar to me, but I didn't know how.

I set Cherios down, and the rabbit hopped along in front of us. I chuckled. How often does one traipse through a garden trailing a white rabbit and holding a child's hand? If I didn't know any better, I'd think I had died and gone to heaven, but I felt quite alive and quite sane.

We marched one behind the other through the garden until we came to a waterfall. The cool spray tingled on my arms and face.

The children gathered in front of me and sang again. This time I sensed visualization from their words, as if they were communicating to me in pictures rather than in language.

The utter inadequacy of speaking with words struck me. The interconnectedness of the living didn't need words. I felt and perceived at a deeper level. It wasn't only the children singing, it was the garden, the waterfall, the flowers, the animals, the birds—every living creature and non-living thing joined together in oneness.

Shale said she had visited the king's garden. Now I understood what she meant. Yeshua said he would be in paradise—this day, to the man on the cross. Was he here somewhere in the garden?

After the children finished, we walked past the waterfall until the trail stopped at a sandy white beach. The beach stretched across an open area to a body of water. A gentle breeze drifted by mingled with the freshness of cleansing water.

Fond memories from my trips to the Red Sea as a young boy stirred within me. I loved to swim. I quickly removed my sandals. I couldn't wait to feel the sand between my toes.

The children set the kittens down, took off their shoes, and ran ahead of me. I noticed something about their footwear. They were old. Everything about the children was perfect—their hair, their faces, their clothing, their voices—they were perfect in every way. Why would they wear old shoes? Then I knew—these were the shoes the children wore on the train.

The girl on the train who had held the star of David wasn't here.

Only those who had held a kitten on the train were here. They had brought their kittens with them.

I traipsed through the sand carrying my sandals. Soon the children made a large circle around me. Not knowing what to do, I bowed several times. They giggled, delightfully entertained. The children glanced upwards and I followed their eyes.

Overhead, hundreds of angels covered the heavens. Several floated down and stood beside me. The children gathered around and clung to them, as if they were guardians.

An angel spoke. "That way," he said to me. "Across the water."

I followed the angel's gaze. On the other side of the river, a castle stood. The citadel on top of the high mountain was the same one I had seen so many times in my dream. I stared at it for a second, speechless. Was my father here?

When I finally started to speak, before I could say anything, the children waved, and then all of them were gone.

CHAPTER 46

My feet sunk in the sand as I ran towards the shoreline. The reflective water rippled back and forth. Along the bottom of the glassy river, golden nuggets sparkled. Overhead, a bird circled and then swooped down, landing at the water's edge. The magnificent creature was more than a bird. He spoke to my mind. "Give me your bag."

The bag had been with me since I discovered the scroll in the temple. Shale's golden nugget and special perfume were in it, as well as the apple Mark gave me that I had yet to eat. Giving the bird my bag made me feel uneasy, but what choice did I have? I couldn't swim with the bag on my shoulder. The water would destroy the precious contents.

I lifted the bag to the bird-like creature. He took hold of it with his beak and flew off. I watched as he soared in a magnificent arc towards the castle.

Anticipation shot up inside me. Was my father really here in the garden?

After taking off my outer robe, I stepped into the water. The temperature felt refreshingly comfortable—not too hot and not too cold. When the water reached my waist, I dove in. A pink dolphin came up alongside. He playfully nudged me and uttered high-pitched squeaks for which dolphins are famous. I wished I knew what he was telling me.

The creature circled and kept me company across the river. When I reached the shore, he looped around once more, as if to say good-bye. Then he awarded me with a graceful arc above the water before swimming away.

I sloshed out of the water onto the sandy beach and let the excess water drip from my shorts. How could the castle be here in the garden? It seemed out of place—everything else was perfect.

The castle was gloomy and dark, except for the bright light emanating from inside and the semitransparent globe that floated beside it. A sense of foreboding crept into my thoughts.

As I began my ascent, the lighted sphere glowing beside the castle moved. I stopped to see what it would do next. I had never seen it change position.

The bright object hovered out over the water and landed near me in the sand. I waited for something to happen. Then the sphere disappeared. Shale stood in front of me, smiling broadly.

What an unexpected surprise. I ran up to greet her. "Strange meeting you here," I blurted out.

She laughed. "You are wet. Would you like a towel and dry clothes?"

I glanced at her hands. Where did she get my clothes? I tried to remember what I wore three years ago. I hoped this meant I was returning to 2015.

"Where are we?" I asked.

Shale laughed. "We're in the seventh dimension—as we used to call it, outside of time, in the king's garden. You must go inside the castle—to understand."

Shale's long brown hair shone with extraordinary brilliance. I was almost at a loss for words. "Will you go with me—inside the castle?"

Shale shook her head. "I would if I could."

I admired her natural beauty. "You are so beautiful."

"Thank you."

"Will—will you wait for me?" I asked.

"I will wait for you, but it won't be in the way you think."

I didn't understand. "When will I see you again?"

Shale smiled. "It's enough to know you will see me again."

I felt cold in my wet clothes and suddenly self-conscious about my appearance.

I reached over and grabbed the towel and other things. "Where should I change?"

Shale pointed to the castle on the mountaintop. "Inside the entrance on the left is a room you can use."

"In my dream, the doors were always locked."

"They won't be locked," Shale promised.

I wanted to talk more, but I was starting to shiver and didn't know what else to say. "I suppose this is it, huh?"

Shale's eyes glistened, as if she was crying. "Things will never be as I once thought, but God's plans are better. I love you, Daniel, in a way you will someday understand more deeply."

What did that mean?

Shale continued. "Finish the journey. The king needs you to finish."

I longed to hug her one more time, but when I started to, she backed away. I respected her feelings. This wasn't the right moment, and I was dripping wet.

"Oh, wait a minute," I exclaimed. "I have something to give you."

Shale's eyes popped wide. "What's that?"

I glanced up at the sky. "The bird has my bag. It's in my bag." Then I remembered Shale's scrolls that I had hidden near the Dead Sea. "I should have kept your scrolls, but I didn't know—"

Shale held up her hands. "Daniel, finish the race Yeshua has set before you. That's all that matters. And I promise, you will see me again."

"All right."

The bright sphere reappeared, and Shale stepped away from me. She waved once more. I waved back, and before I knew it, she was gone.

A few seconds later, the sphere gently lifted and returned to the castle in its familiar position. I smiled. Maybe she was watching me. I needed to finish, she said. I had heard that expression many times in sports—finish the game. You can't win if you don't finish.

I began the steep climb up the mountain. Of course, I had every intention of finishing. Compared to rappelling, the climb up the mountain was easier. Perspective was everything. My shoulder no longer hurt, which surprised me.

Still, I was out of breath at the halfway point. I stopped to survey the garden below me, but clouds blocked my view. At least snow wasn't falling, and my hands weren't frostbitten.

Did they have four seasons here in the king's garden? I couldn't imagine it ever getting cold here—or rainy or stormy. I laughed. They probably didn't even need meteorologists.

Once I reached the top, I cautiously drew near the dark gated entrance to the castle. The door opened automatically. The winged creature was waiting for me and held my bag in his beak. I reached out and took it. "Thank you."

He spoke a few strange words, although I didn't know what he said this time. Then he flew away.

For the first time since arriving, fear gripped me. Perhaps it seemed worse because I didn't expect it. I remembered one of the Psalms I had read at Brutus Snyder's home. "Though I walk through the valley of the shadow of death, I will fear no evil, for thou art with me."

Even if this wasn't a valley, the words still helped to ease my anxiety.

I entered through the Roman archway and into a covered portico. When I pushed the gate forward, the door groaned, as if it hadn't been opened in a long time. I timidly peered inside.

Everything looked the same—the long, arched hallway with many doors on each side of the corridor, the torches flickering along the high walls—even the mosaic of Mount Everest. At the end of the dark foyer, wooden stairs led to the second floor. At the top was a large door. I hoped to find my father on the other side of that door.

Unexpectedly, again, fear clawed at me, like a savage beast, overshadowing my elation. I repeated the words, "I will fear no evil, for thou art with me."

I walked over to the left side of the entranceway as Shale had instructed and turned the handle of the first door. To my surprise, it opened.

I entered into a bathroom exquisitely decorated in gold trim. The huge antique mirrors caught my attention. I rushed over to examine my face. I looked the same, but maybe it was because I hadn't seen myself in a mirror in three years.

I lifted my hair. There it was—the mark, in the shape of a cross. Perhaps it was a tattoo. No, it wasn't a tattoo. I didn't know what it was. I pressed down on it. How had I received it? And my brother had one, too. He must be my brother from 2015.

We knew Jacob was on a secret assignment, but assumed it had to do with the military. We weren't allowed to know his whereabouts. I had always thought it strange that it happened so suddenly. Only Martha knew his secret location.

I quickly changed into the dry clothes Shale had brought me and walked back out into the corridor. Again, fear cried out in brutal, assaulting attacks. I prayed once more, "Though I walk through the valley of the shadow of death, I will fear no evil, for thou art with me."

Before I could climb the stairs, a power I didn't understand blocked me. Was God speaking? All I wanted to do was rescue my father.

I tried once more to ascend the stairs when suddenly a child appeared on the steps in front of me—the young girl from the train, the one I sensed I recognized, but I didn't know from where.

She pointed towards the door. "Go there," she said, and then she disappeared.

Why couldn't I rescue my father first?

I reluctantly walked over and turned the handle of the first door on the left side. The door swung open.

When I entered, I stepped into another dimension. Only this time I was a spectator. I was on a train—the same one on which I traveled to Jerusalem. Young hands stroked kittens. The girl I recognized clutched the Star of David. The train chugged. Oppressive heat stung my face, and thick smoke billowed outside the steel windows, terrorizing the passengers.

The man gagged the woman until she quit screaming. Soft moans escaped from the children—the children I had seen in the garden—and moms tried to shield their innocent eyes.

The train stopped beside a large sign. I peered out—in big, bold letters on a rustic sign was the word "Auschwitz." A Nazi soldier ordered everyone out. He had a huge dog beside him—enough to scare anyone who tried to escape.

I never knew what happened because the train dissipated the first time. Now I watched as the men went in one direction, the women and children in another. I listened as the official read off the names.

I heard my grandmother's name. The young girl with the necklace stepped forward.

My great grandparents died in the gas chambers. It was the photograph of my mother's grandparents that my mother kept by her bedside. My mother's mother, the young girl, should have died as the rest did. Someone must have befriended her.

When I examined her hand more closely, I recognized the Star of David—as the one in my bag. I trembled unexpectedly and ran out of the room.

In the hallway, I struggled to catch my breath. The holocaust and I were linked in a way I didn't understand. Was it because I feared it could happen again? The holocaust had crippled my mother emotionally, as if she must bear the scars of the hellish past so no one would forget.

Was I wounded also? Was it now part of my Jewish psyche? Was there nothing that could heal the biting memories that tormented my people?

Fear swept over me. I prayed again, "Though I walk through the valley of the shadow of death, I will fear no evil."

I started to run up the stairs, but another young girl stopped me. She walked down the steps, took my hand, and led me to one of the doors. She waited for me to open it. I turned the handle and walked into the room.

My family sat at the table. Everyone was there—my father; my mother; Martha, my sister; Jacob, my brother; and me. We all held hands as my father said the blessing.

I looked down at the young girl who had held my hand when I arrived in the garden. She continued to hold it as my father prayed.

I asked her softly, "What is your name?"

"Mari," she replied,

When the prayer was over, she faded away.

If Mari was my sister in the first century, she must be my sister in 2015. Why had I never met her? The room darkened and the scene dissipated. I walked back out into the long hallway and wept.

Fear returned and the foreboding increased. When I returned home, I must learn the truth. I must know the truth about Mari.

When I had gathered myself, I started to go up the stairs again to rescue my father. Surely nothing would stop me now. I climbed the first step, and Lilly stood on a step a few feet above me.

She shook her head. "Not yet." She pointed towards another door and then disappeared.

Only one more door—please, God, only one more door. I ran over and turned the handle and entered the room. I saw myself walking briskly through Jerusalem, returning home from the Family and Youth Treatment Center.

A voice called to me, "Daniel."

Lilly offered me the New Testament. I took it reluctantly. I treated the book with disdain, at first refusing to bring it into the house. When I did later, in the middle of the night, I hid it under my pillow, embarrassed that someone might find it. How foolish and stupid I was. Why was I so afraid to own a New Testament?

I rushed back out into the hallway. I had seen enough. I didn't want to open another door. All I wanted to do was rescue my father. I started to run up the stairs when Shale appeared on the steps in front of me.

"Daniel," she said.

I trembled, unable to speak.

"Just one more door," she spoke gently. "Sometimes we must go through many doors to prepare us to enter the most important one."

Then she faded from my presence.

Haltingly, I walked to next door and turned the knob. Another vision from the past spread before me. I watched as Shale arrived on a donkey. How silly I appeared, so overcome with her beauty.

Shale repeatedly tried to share her faith. When I rejected Yeshua, I rejected her. She loved the king more than anything else—more than her parents, more than riches, more than fame, more than life itself. I buried my face in my hands and wept. How could I have been so foolish?

I ran out into the hallway. I couldn't bring myself to open any more doors. Please, God, no more doors. Please let me rescue my father. All my thoughts focused on him. I didn't want to be shown any more from my past—a past filled with mistakes and shortcomings.

I climbed the stairs. I would tell my father how much I loved him. I continued climbing one step at a time. I would offer to trade places with him. The stairs creaked as I got closer to the top. I would set him free. I wanted my life to have value. I wanted to think I mattered. I wanted my life to count—to be worth something.

At last I reached the top of the stairs. I turned the handle and the huge door swung open. But I didn't see my father chained to the wall. I saw someone else.

CHAPTER 47

Yeshua sat on a throne decorated lavishly in gold. Next to him was a plain wooden chair with severe edges. I recognized the chair as the one I sat in when my journey began. My Savior was dressed in a white luminous robe and a golden shining crown covered his head.

He appeared to be waiting for someone. Books covered all four walls of the room and extended upwards as far as I could see. A small fire burned in a stone fireplace.

Yeshua's joy filled the room. I had never seen him so content, so radiant, so untroubled. His beaming eyes met mine and pierced my heart.

I clutched the door handle. "I'm sorry to disturb you," I stammered. "I thought someone else was in here."

Yeshua waved his hand at the empty chair. "Please come in and sit with me."

I closed the door and stumbled into the room. I was not worthy of sitting beside him. Instead, I knelt—and wept.

After a moment, Yeshua touched me. A tingling sensation swept through my body. While I expected condemnation, I received love—unmeasured, freely flowing, and complete.

I lifted my head and whispered, "I'm sorry."

He waved his hand again at the chair. "Daniel, please, sit in the chair. I have much to tell you."

I stood and sat next to him. My eyes fell on Yeshua's face. His appearance was astonishingly similar to when he was on earth, but a supernatural element made him so much more. He was not just an ordinary man. He was God's son, the son of man, as foretold in the Hebrew writings. I glanced down at his hands—the scars from the crucifixion covered his wrists. Would the scars be there forever?

What do you say to the king of kings? No words came forth as I sat stunned and tongue-tied.

Yeshua spoke first. "Daniel, tell me, what do you see?"

I glanced around the room. I had never seen so many books—thousands of them. The room had no ceiling—it was as if the books reached up into heaven, or we were in heaven.

"I see books, my Lord."

Yeshua smiled, "These aren't ordinary books."

An angel walked into the room carrying some food and drinks on a platter. He set the tray down on the table.

"Thank you," Yeshua said.

The angel bowed and left us.

The king said a prayer in Hebrew. Then he broke the bread and handed me a piece. I waited for him to take the first bite.

After eating the bread, Yeshua spoke again. "Daniel, do you have that scroll from the temple?"

I pulled the scroll out of my bag and handed it to him.

Yeshua opened it. "This is your life, Daniel, recorded from beginning to end. Only I can break the seal." He smiled reassuringly. "The evil one has lost the battle for your soul."

At that moment, I remembered the wager between the light and dark creatures who had fought over me. How had I forgotten something so important?

"The battle was always mine," Yeshua said. "I know who wins."

"Is it always like that?" I asked.

"Everyone must choose. I died for all, but you must believe I died for you—for your transgressions."

"Why did I find the scroll in the temple?"

"You ask good questions, Daniel. The evil one wanted your soul. He tried to take it—many times. You learned from your mistakes. The value of one's life is immeasurable in the kingdom of God.

"Human life is precious—so precious that I gave my life. Even if it was only your life, Daniel, and no one else who needed to be saved, I would have died for you. When you found the scroll, it was as if you were finding your life in me."

I swallowed hard as tears filled my eyes. I couldn't fathom that kind of love. Would I ever be able to understand?

Yeshua waved his hand at the books. "These are the lives of the saints —those who believe in me. In each book is recorded the person's deeds, his or her stories—the life of the individual from beginning to end. All the wonderful things the saints did in my name are remembered forever."

Yeshua stood and walked over to the wall by the fireplace. He put my book on the bookshelf and then rejoined me.

"Do you understand?" he asked.

I feared answering incorrectly. "A little bit."

Yeshua leaned towards me. "Look around. At the Judgment Seat, I will open the books and reward each person for what he has done in my name."

I wiped tears from my eyes.

"You have many questions, Daniel. Let me see if I can answer some of them."

"Thank you, my Lord. If I may ask one question of you about my father, is he alive?"

Yeshua's eyes reassured me. "You entered this room hoping to rescue your father."

"Yes, sir."

"If you trust in me, I will help you to rescue him."

"I will trust in you."

Yeshua added, "But it won't be easy."

"I believe you."

"When you return home, the world will be different. Study the Scriptures, both the Old and New Testaments. Remember, you are not fighting against flesh and blood, but against principalities. The evil one holds your father, but I have overcome the world."

I nodded.

Yeshua leaned towards me. "People have hated me from the beginning and have always hated me without cause—without reason."

I had witnessed that. Even the religious leaders, like the council, whom I would have expected to love Yeshua the most, had hated him.

"You will face much persecution. Perilous times are ahead." Yeshua peered into my eyes. "Stay true to me. The word of our heavenly Father remains forever."

I asked in my heart for understanding as I listened to Yeshua's words.

Yeshua sighed. "Some have tried to discredit me speaking worthless words and false oaths. Others have tried to imitate me with false miracles. Many have done good things to glorify themselves and not me. They have already received their reward. False doctrines abound. Most live in spiritual darkness, preferring the comforts of this world rather than sacrificing for the next. The evil one lurks and snatches up those who have strayed. A day of judgment is coming."

Yeshua studied me. "And many will seek to destroy you."

I nodded.

"But fear not. If you stay close to me, I will give you the desires of your heart, including the rescue of your father."

My heart thumped with unspeakable joy.

Yeshua spoke with unwavering authority. "I have chosen one hundred forty-four thousand Jews. I have sanctified and sealed them for a divine purpose. All the young men are virgins. They will be the greatest evangelists the world has ever seen. You are one of them."

Was Yeshua speaking to me? I wanted to look around the room and make sure he wasn't speaking to someone else, but no one was present but me. Then I remembered the times I had been tempted—and the time the demon had tried to seduce me. I touched my forehead with a shaky hand. "Is this the seal?"

"Yes. Do not be afraid. I hold your life in my hands."

I couldn't believe Yeshua had chosen me for anything.

I am giving you your first special assignment for the kingdom of heaven.

"You are?"

"Let's pray first."

After we finished praying, Yeshua said, "Angels are everywhere on the earth doing my bidding. You will seem as one of them when you return. Someone is in desperate need. You will heal him through my power."

I nodded, trying to understand.

Yeshua emphasized, "Again, the time is short. We do not wrestle against flesh and blood, but against principalities, against powers, against the rulers of darkness, against spiritual hosts of wickedness. I will be with you always, until the end."

"Thank you, my Lord."

"Let's finish our meal," Yeshua said. "I will share a few more truths with you before you return home."

CHAPTER 48

Wednesday, May 19, 1948

I stood in the darkness. My only light came from a couple of fires that refused to die. The Arabs had set fire to the buildings in the Jewish Quarter. Most of the synagogues were in ruins and our holy places desecrated. The Arabs cared nothing about our heritage, but then, in a war, who cares about anything but winning? The hospital had escaped the worst of it, thanks to a shift in the winds, but I knew the reprieve was only temporary.

I walked inside the "emergency" room of Synagogue Hall. It reminded me of another "emergency" room in 2015. The room was crowded with mattresses. The staff had laid many patients on the dirty floor. There was no other place to put them. A small oil lamp provided the only light.

I searched for my mentor and friend. In order for General Goren to save Jerusalem in the future, Yeshua needed me to save his life now. I found the young man in a dark corner. Next to him was a nurse who had fallen asleep. Two doctors had performed surgery a few hours earlier. There was little hope that he would survive, but with Yeshua, all things are possible.

I approached my mentor, nervously brushing my hair away from my forehead. Then I remembered General Goren's words on his deathbed. He said he saw my scar. I reached over and touched his chest. "In the name of Yeshua, I pray God will restore you to health and save your life this very hour."

General Goren didn't have the strength to respond. I lingered for a few moments with my head bowed. I leaned on his bed, thinking about all I had learned, all that I had seen, and all that Yeshua the Messiah had told me.

When I opened my eyes, things were different. I was in the same place—sixty-seven years into the future.

The bed I was leaning on was empty. Sirens blared outside. I glanced across the hallway. The door I once saw no longer existed. And there was no strange light shining through the tiny window. That was the beginning of my journey. Now I was at the end. I had to stop and remember—what had I come out into the hallway to do? Beds, the doctor had asked me to bring in more beds.

I took the mattress I was leaning on and pushed it through the door. Once it was out of the way of foot traffic, I walked over to check on Lilly's father. Warm memories of meeting his daughter in the seventh dimension returned, but those thoughts quickly faded when I saw his bed was empty—except for his clothes. How strange. They appeared so similar to Yeshua's burial cloth—but where was Lilly's father?

I ran up to the nurse and pointed to his bed. "Did the man pass away or get moved to somewhere else?"

"No," she replied. "A few of our patients have disappeared. We can't find them.

NEXT BOOK IN SEVENTH DIMENSION SERIES

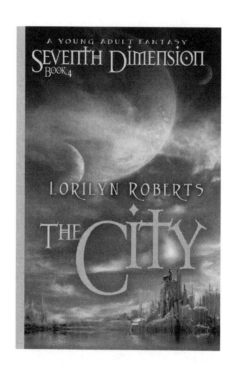

LorilynRoberts.com

Children of Dreams

As an Audiobook

Tails and Purrs for the Heart and Soul

As an Audiobook

THE DONKEY AND THE KING
(A Story of Redemption)

Lorilyn Roberts
Illustrated by Linda S. DiFranco

Look for the hidden word "good" on every page.

The Donkey and the King: A Story of Redemption

"Wonderful story with positive Christian values. Loved the illustrations. It's a hit with my kids!"

—"Goodreads" reader

Young readers become world leaders.

Book Love

"Book Love is beautiful inside and out. Roberts uses a child to teach children the love of books and it works beautifully. This book is a must for elementary classrooms and libraries. I highly recommend Book Love by Lorilyn Roberts if you have a child wanting to learn to read."

—Joy Hannabass, Readers' Favorite Reviewer

SEVENTH DIMENSION SERIES

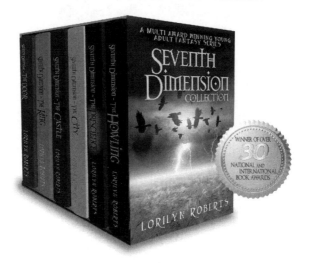

LorilynRoberts.com

Seventh Dimension - The Door, Book 1

As an Audiobook

Seventh Dimension - The King, Book 2

As an Audiobook

Seventh Dimension - The Castle, Book 3

As an Audiobook

Seventh Dimension - The City, Book 4

As an Audiobook

Seventh Dimension - The Prescience, Book 5

Audiobook coming

Seventh Dimension - The Howling, Book 6

As an Audiobook

ADDITIONAL BOOKS

LorilynRoberts.com

Food for Thought Cookbook

Seventh Dimension Devotional Series: Am I Okay, God?

Born-Again Jews - companion book to *Seventh Dimension - The King* - coming

ABOUT THE AUTHOR

When not writing books, Lorilyn provides closed captioning for television. She adopted her two daughters from Nepal and Vietnam as a single mother and lives in Florida with many rescued cats and a dog.

Lorilyn has won over thirty-five awards for the *Seventh Dimension Series*. She graduated Magna Cum Laude from the University of Alabama with a bachelor's degree in social sciences/humanities that included an emphasis in Biblical history and on-site study in Jerusalem. She received her Master of Arts in Creative Writing from Perelandra College. In her spare time, she is also a ham radio operator. KO4LBS.

Visit Lorilyn's website at LorilynRoberts.com to learn more about her books.

If you enjoyed this book, please consider posting a short review on your favorite book-related website. Reviews help authors a great deal, and they are the best way to spread the news about a book.

Thank you for your interest and support.

RESOURCES USED IN WRITING THIS BOOK
BOOKS AND ARTICLES

*The Day He Died, The Passion According to Luke,*by Matthew Byrne

A Visual Guide to Gospel Events, Fascinating Insights into Where They Happened and Why by James C. Martin, John A. Beck, and David G. Hansen

Jewish New Testament Commentary by David H. Stern

Answering Jewish Objections to Jesus Volumes 1, 2, and 3 by Michael L. Brown

The Last Days of Jesus, by Bill O'Reilly

Women Who Knew The Mortal Messiah by Heather Horrocks

Pontius Pilate, A Novel by Paul L. Maier

Night by Elie Wiesel

Man's Search for Meaning by Viktor E. Frankl

http://www.cbn.com/spirituallife/biblestudyandtheology/jewishroots/amidah_prayer_bivin.aspx?option=print

http://www.bible-history.com/jewishtemple/JEWISH_TEMPLESchematic_Plan_of_the_Temple.htm

http://www.hebrew4christians.com/Holidays/Spring_Holidays/Shabbat_HaGadol/shabbat_hagadol.html

https://www.youtube.com/watch?v=f6nKDZhMono

https://www.jewishvirtuallibrary.org/jsource/judaica/ejud_0002_0014_0_14119.html

http://josephus.org/Passover.htm

http://www.mycrandall.ca/courses/NTintro/JerusalTempl4.htm

http://www.cbcg.org/studies_templemount.htm

http://www.jesuscentral.com/ji/historical-jesus/jesus-final_week.php

http://www.agapebiblestudy.com/documents/Jesus%20Last%20Week%20in%20Jerusalem.htm

https://en.wikipedia.org/wiki/Second_Temple

http://www.biblicalarchaeology.org/daily/biblical-sites-places/jerusalem/hezekiah%E2%80%99s-tunnel-reexamined/

http://www.jewishencyclopedia.com/articles/11934-passover-sacrifice

http://www.generationword.com/jerusalem101/18-gihon-springs.html

http://templemountlocation.com/fortAntonia.html

https://www.templeinstitute.org/passover.htm

http://www.reasonablefaith.org/the-triumphal-entry

http://www.bible-history.com/maps/ancient-roads-in-israel.html

https://www.youtube.com/watch?v=nHUPeDSqjsg

http://www.bible-history.com/jerusalem/firstcenturyjerusalem_antonia_fortress.html

http://www.ensignmessage.com/archives/mysteriousevents.html

http://www.egrc.net/articles/other/amidah.html

http://www.ein-gedi.co.il/fr/?p=66

http://www.gospel-mysteries.net/mary-magdalene.html

http://www.bible-archaeology.info/index.htm

http://www.bible-history.com/jerusalem/firstcenturyjerusalem_golden_gate.html

http://www.leaderu.com/everystudent/easter/articles/josh2.html

https://www.templeinstitute.org/passover.htm

http://www.jewishvoice.org/media/publications/articles/ten-biggest-lies-about-yeshua.html

http://www.hebrew4christians.com/Holidays/Spring_Holidays/Shabbat_HaGadol/shabbat_hagadol.html

http://www.templemount.org/TMTRS.html

http://jesusalive.cc/ques220.htm

http://templemountlocation.com/fortAntonia.html

https://www.youtube.com/watch?v=HHLD6RXVLaM

http://goodnewspirit.com/footnote_perpetualsacrifice.htm

https://www.jewishvirtuallibrary.org/jsource/Judaism/Sanhedrin.html

http://biblepropheciesfulfilled.blogspot.com/2015/03/sacrifices-being-performed-at-rebuilt.html?showComment=1426480902110#c1805950372677765551

https://www.youtube.com/watch?v=YNmERZkT6JM

https://www.biblegateway.com/resources/all-women-bible/Mary-Magdalene